TOP GUN

FROM THE 1986 BLOCKBUSTER TO *MAVERICK*

UP IN THE AIR & BEHIND THE SCENES

THE *PEOPLE* INTERVIEW
Tom Cruise talks flying, films and more (see page 16).

★ CONTENTS ★

FACE FORWARD
Cruise in 1986's *Top Gun*. "I always trained with helmets and pads," says the actor, who went helmet-free so an audience will "feel what the character is going through."

★ AN ALL-NEW ★
TOP GUN

AN INSIDE LOOK AT THE SEQUEL, THE CAST OF YOUNG FLIERS AND WHAT IT TOOK FOR TOM CRUISE TO RETURN TO MOVIE THEATERS AS 'MAVERICK' AFTER MORE THAN THREE DECADES

ON CLOUD 9
"There's a beauty to flight," says Cruise (as Maverick in the new film). "That pursuit of flight—to be able to build these machines…and to be able to do it."

★ *TOP GUN: MAVERICK* ★

READY FOR TAKEOFF

AFTER 36 YEARS, CAPT. PETE 'MAVERICK' MITCHELL RETURNS—IN A CHANGED WORLD

A LOT OF PEOPLE WORKED for many years to deliver a sequel to *Top Gun*. To take nothing away from the filmmakers' long-held vision, the idea that there should be a follow-up to 1986's highest-earning film is a no-brainer. The potent combination of daredevil aerial action, romantic tension, personal sacrifice, hot bods playing ball on the beach and boozy bar singing never gets old. Neither, it seems, does star Tom Cruise who, in fact, turns 60 in 2022 and is (as his Instagram bio reminds us) still running in movies. But despite a desire for another chapter—on the part of fans, studio execs and Cruise himself—decades passed without one. And then, in 2019, he turned up to reveal a trailer at Comic-Con in San Diego, down the street from where *Top Gun*'s piano bar scenes had been shot 34 years before. At last, the sequel was due out in the summer of 2020. And then... yeah, 2020. The release pushed back to the end of 2021. And again... never mind. But now *Top Gun: Maverick* is arriving, and on these pages *People* has a look at the film in which Capt. Pete "Maverick" Mitchell returns to the TOPGUN naval aviator school as an instructor for a young squad of elite pilots. This Maverick has a few more frequent flier miles on him, and the world and the Navy have changed. (In real life too: In 1993 women were cleared to fly combat missions, a welcome bit of equality reflected in the new film.) There are new faces, new planes, new challenges. But some things don't change. Is it a spoiler to suggest that if you loved what made *Top Gun Top Gun,* you are likely to be happy with the sequel? There will be familiar tunes, scenes to ignite generational nostalgia, grown men and women with nicknames and, of course, there will be flying. "It's a celebration of aviation and a look into what it feels like to be an F-18 pilot today," Cruise tells *People*. (His full interview, page 16.) "Through all the films that we made, we're able to use all of our knowledge to give the audience that experience." Fasten your seat belts!

FLYBOYS
At left: Three of the young pilots Tom Cruise's Maverick must whip into elite shape (from left): Greg Tarzan Davis as Coyote; Glen Powell as Hangman and Jack Schumacher as Omaha.

LIFE LESSONS
Below: Maverick instructs his charges—as Cruise did off-camera (see page 42 to go behind the scenes). "I learned so much more about the craft of film acting than I could have ever learned in a classroom," says Davis.

> WHEN I WAS A KID, I SAW *TOP GUN* ON TV . . . AND I JUST REMEMBER THINKING, 'MAN, THESE GUYS LOOK COOL.'"
> —MILES TELLER, 'ROOSTER'

SON OF A GUN
Miles Teller (above) as Bradley "Rooster" Bradshaw, son of Maverick's best friend, Goose (Anthony Edwards), from the original *Top Gun*.

TOP BRASS
Jon Hamm, who plays hard-nosed air boss Adm. Beau "Cyclone" Simpson and Charles Parnell as Adm. Solomon "Warlock" Bates. "Jon is kind of 'sneaky funny,'" Parnell says of working with the *Mad Men* star.

NEW BLOOD
"You take off, and it's beautiful and majestic; you could see for miles, and it's everything you would expect it to be," says Jay Ellis, who plays Payback (center above, with Danny Ramirez as Fanboy, and Monica Barbaro as Phoenix), of flying.

ON THE CARPET
"He's an awesome scene partner, I'll tell you that much," Hamm says of Cruise (with him and Parnell). "He's always prepared. He's always on time. He's excellent, as we all know."

"IT FELT LIKE SUMMER CAMP. WHEN WE HAD DAYS OFF, ALL ACTIVITIES WERE GROUP PLANNED. . . . IT TRULY FEELS LIKE A DREAM NOW BECAUSE IT'S SO LONG AGO"

—DANNY RAMIREZ, 'FANBOY'

PLAYING WITH THE BOYS
In an updated nod to the volleyball scene in *Top Gun,* the pilot trainees have a game of football on the beach.

PLANE MAN
Above: Cruise, in character. "He has no ego; he just wants the best from everybody," says Teller. "He's not worried about shining through. He's the first one there, the last to leave."

'PHOENIX' AT EASE
Barbaro recalls seeing the first *Top Gun* and thinking "it was just one of those movies that really makes you want to be a part of that thing—whatever it is—just the beauty of filmmaking."

WINGMEN
Ramirez (with Ellis, opposite) admits he "was starstruck" working with Cruise, Hamm and Ed Harris. "But the transition to seeing them as just people was really easy."

INTO THE SPIN CYCLE
"Scariest thing about the training," says Lewis Pullman, who plays Bob (with Barbaro), "was feeling like you're a cat in a drying machine, being tossed around and trying not to puke."

> "I felt, working with Tom, like he never took anything for granted. . . . He really just gives everything his all, all the time"
> —JENNIFER CONNELLY

UNDER THE HOOD
Maverick performs a little plane maintenance in the film—one of the few particulars Cruise didn't need to tend to on-set. "He's so detail-oriented," says Glen Powell ("Hangman"). "I think that's what a good pilot is, or at least what makes a safe pilot."

FREE-WHEELING
Maverick out for a spin. “I didn’t have a lot of crazy stunt stuff to do,” says Jon Hamm. “I like doing that stuff fine, but I think very few people in the universe like it in the way that Tom likes it.”

LOVE INTEREST
“I think it makes sense that they keep finding themselves in each other’s lives,” Jennifer Connelly (below) says of her character, Penny, who has a recurring relationship with Cruise’s Pete Mitchell.

BACK AT IT
Cruise in the title role of *Top Gun: Maverick.*

THE *PEOPLE* INTERVIEW

TOM CRUISE ★ AS ★ MAVERICK

'I WAS THE KID WHO WOULD SNEAK OUT MY WINDOW, CLIMB UP ON THE ROOF AND LOOK AT THE STARS.' THE ACTOR ON TWO LIFELONG PASSIONS: FLYING AND FILMMAKING (AND WHY HE DOESN'T NEED TO SPEED)

TOM CRUISE has, after 40 years of making movies, earned the right to rest on his laurels—or at least on his couch. His films have grossed more than $10 billion. He's a triple-Oscar-nominated leading man who does his own stunts: hangs from planes, rides choppers off cliffs, leaps across rooftops (breaking his ankle in one instance but not his stride). His decision to reprise the character who proved, 36 summers ago, that Cruise could open a blockbuster now puts the weight of *Top Gun: Maverick*'s success on the star's shoulders. Yet on the eve of his 60th birthday, he shows no signs of taking a pause—or even a nap. The only topic that seems to make him weary (or tip off his age) is promotion. "It used to be, I remember a marketing meeting, there'd be three networks," says Cruise. "Now it's like you have all these different Twitters and 20 different channels and... oh my God." For someone so committed to pushing into the future—he has plans to shoot a film on the International Space Station—he can be surprisingly sentimental about the past. Early in his career he bristled at press tours that lasted months. "I was like, 'I can't do it. Please, let's just set up a huge premiere.' I grew up watching those Grauman's Chinese premieres. Remember those great black-and-white photos of James Dean and [Paul] Newman?" He pitched studios the idea of holding fewer but bigger, more glamorous events in overseas markets, saying, he recalls, "'Let's bring Hollywood to the world. Let's make it *fun*.'" That remains a guiding principle for Cruise and one reason that, when *People* caught up with him, he was in South Africa, flying helicopters and filming *Mission Impossible 8*. Cruise graciously took a break from the fun stuff to speak with editor Allison Adato.

What drew you back to *Top Gun*?

TOM CRUISE For decades, people have been asking. The germ of the idea actually originated back in '86, '87. Obviously, I was too young at that stage to do it. At a certain point we're doing *Fallout* [the 2018 *Mission Impossible* film], and... it coalesced. I thought, "If I'm ever going to do it, let's go for it now."

Was there something about the character that you wanted to revisit?

It wasn't so much about wanting to revisit a character. I don't feel that way. I was thinking of audiences. I started realizing, "Oh, look at the effects and what we would be able to give to an audience this time."

Why was having real flying crucial?

Even when I did *Top Gun* the first time, I said, "Look, if I do this, I want to shoot it for real in the F-14. You've got to film me in it." I always wanted to give that audience that experience. How do we do this in a manner that becomes about character and story and put the audience in that emotional framework?

How do you?

It was incredibly complicated! I had to teach the actors not only how to fly... I had to teach the fighter pilots how to get a performance within that. The studio thought it would have made sense to shoot the aerial stuff first. I kept saying, "Guys, it's impossible. You can't do it." They just kept saying it. I said, "Okay. I tell you what—we'll take one day, and we'll do a test." Sometimes people have to experience it themselves. We did the flight, and everything that could go wrong went wrong. Everyone said, "Let's pump the brakes. Okay, Tom, I get it. This is challenging."

When things go wrong with planes, one might think: tragedy. Clearly that's not what happened.

No. It was just things like the camera in the wrong place. The footage we got was spectacular, but it was also something where we go, "We can do

STEPPING UP
Cruise as Maverick and (opposite) with Miles Teller in the film.

SEE TOM RUN
"He treats himself like an athlete—the way he eats, trains, rests his body," producer Jerry Bruckheimer says of Cruise (above and left, in 2018's *Mission Impossible: Fallout*). "Even though he's in his 50s, he's more like a 30-year-old. I'd put him up against anybody."

THE EARLY SHOW
Right: Cruise visited 2019 Comic-Con with a trailer for *Maverick*, a film that, he jokes, "I was working on, I think, for four years? Five years? Thirty years?"

it better." I showed the actors the mistakes that I made in terms of where I was looking at the camera. When you have a limited amount of time and you're pulling G's—no matter what people think—there's a *lot* going on in that airplane. The pilot's there. There's other airplanes. There's camera ships that are coming right up close to you. I'm trying to get everyone into a place where they're not thinking about that stuff as much, so that they can have their performances. Because they're enormously talented people. I wanted their personalities and their characters to come through. I have to perform, and I'm discovering what works for this character. It's an exploration in the same way you cook a meal. Every time, it's a little different, and you have to be willing to tolerate a bit of chaos. You have to have a high level of skill to get to that place where you have the freedom of discovery.

Did you enjoy the role of mentor?
Look, I like seeing people do well. There's a pleasure in seeing them overcome the things that they had to overcome and see them shine. What I try to do is set the table for everyone, where they can succeed, and I'm learning how I can help them. I need their help too. It's a team. I like seeing all the actors, Miles [Teller] and Glen [Powell], each one having their moments. Monica [Barbaro], she could do anything in the airplane. Some people are like that. Women are like that a lot—they don't get sick. They can handle heavy G's. The first time I flew in the F-14, I vomited—I've never gotten sick in an airplane since. Some of the guys were getting sick throughout filming. But they didn't stop. Literally, they would vomit . . . then film.

Most people would have to lie down.
I know. It was intense, but they

knew, “I have 20 minutes to get this shot.” Some of them were embarrassed. I said, “Stop. You are getting it done, and your performances are great.”

Miles Teller mentioned some of the flying was challenging for him.

That [scene] when we’re going up a chute, inverted just a couple of feet off of the rock face—I just want to tell you, Miles is *not* a very comfortable flyer. He never complained. I could see he was terrified, and he did it. I’m going, “My hat is off to you, man.” That character he created, it’s beautiful. I’m grateful to all of them. They all wanted to come on board the adventure.

How was it for you doing that kind of fighter-jet flying again?

Exhilarating. It’s always a great challenge and a privilege to fly with those pilots. I’m not going to lie, I love it up there. I love flight. I’ve been fascinated by it my entire life.

Composer Hans Zimmer asked you to explain your love of flying so he might capture it in the film’s score. What did you tell him?

I wanted it to be a love letter to aviation. Not only the challenges but the beauty. I parachute. I speed fly. I fly helicopters. I fly aerobatics. In all of those forms there’s a poetry about it, where you’re looking at what man is capable of, to see the world from that viewpoint. I’ve flown where I have birds fly right up next to me—we’re flying together. It’s just… it’s beautiful. I was the kid who would sneak out my window, climb up on the roof and look at the stars. So to be in a plane and look at the stars, it’s amazing to me.

There’s a scene where Maverick is challenged about why he hasn’t progressed beyond the rank of captain after 30 years and many commendations. Have there been people in your industry who say, “Yes, you’re this big movie star,

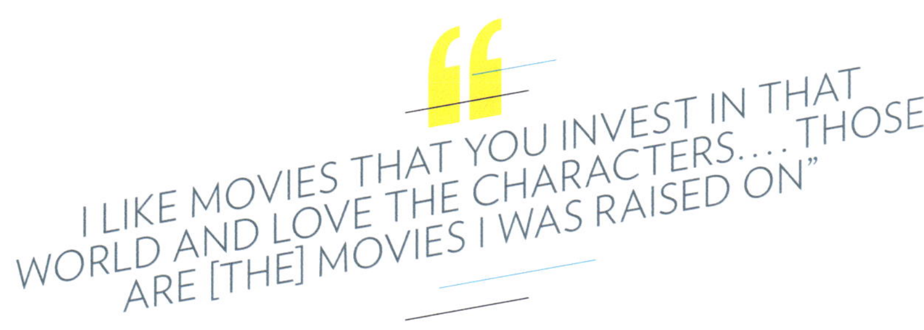

but how come you're not, say, directing?" I'm wondering if that aspect of Maverick resonated.
No. People have all different various opinions, but I've always done exactly what I wanted to do. People have evaluations, and that's okay. I absolutely love what I do.

What was it like to work with Val Kilmer again?
I've always admired his work, his talent. There's stuff that we just, we get together... we just start laughing. It was special to have him back. It meant a lot to me. He's the kind of actor that—even physically the things that he has going on—he's that artist, he's so powerful with even little moments that resonate.

The first film came out in a different era, and not everyone embraced its military theme. Do you feel you have a more receptive audience today?
I always felt universally positive about the military. I always had a lot of respect for what they do, their skill level and their commitment. I didn't feel that aspect then when I did it. Maybe you did. I didn't.

Has a traffic cop ever stopped you and quoted "Need for speed"?
No. I wish they would.

Maybe you never speed?
Sometimes. I get stopped. But also, I spend a lot of time on racetracks, on motorcycles, in helicopters, so I get a lot of that stuff out.

How did it feel to sit in a theater and see *Maverick* finally completed?
When COVID hit, everybody was like, "We're not going to finish *Top Gun*." We were in the middle of an edit! I was like, "Well, yes, we're finishing *Top Gun*. And we're going to start shooting *Mission*." I did a tricky thing and called the other studios, going, "Yeah, we're shooting our movie. How come you're not shooting yours?" Then I called [our] studio and said, "Universal is shooting. How come we're not?" I was like, "People are getting food by Uber..." There's a long pause on the Zoom call. Everyone says, "Yes, food's going." I said, "All I want to do is deliver a mic by Uber." We were dressing people up in hazmat suits, recording musicians in their apartments. Everyone jumped on board. Then to have everyone enjoy it in a big movie theater was—it was wonderful. It was quite emotional for all of us now that we're finally finished.

At the same time, you were starting up two *Mission Impossible* movies. Aren't you exhausted? When was your last vacation?
This *is* my vacation. My whole life, since I was 4 years old, I wanted to make movies. I wanted to fly. I wanted an adventurous life. Suddenly I was 18, and I'm making *Taps* and going, "Oh my gosh, this is really happening!" This is what I love to do. It's challenging and interesting. I get to work with incredible people from all different cultures. It's something I never take for granted. I'm grateful.

Can't you be both grateful *and* exhausted?
Oh, don't think I don't get exhausted. I'm human. I do get exhausted. But I just keep going, you know? ■

THE A TEAM
"She's an incredible actress," says director Joseph Kosinski. "She and Tom have both been working in Hollywood since they were kids and had never been in the same movie."

JENNIFER CONNELLY
★ AS ★
PENNY

AFTER EARNING ACCLAIM FOR DARKER ROLES, THE ACTRESS WAS READY TO TAKE ON *TOP GUN'S* SUNNY SO-CAL LOVE INTEREST (LUCKILY, SHE'D RECENTLY CONQUERED HER FEAR OF FLYING)

BY ERIK FORREST JACKSON

ONCE A CHILD STAR, Jennifer Connelly graduated to make a name for herself in dark and dramatic fare. She earned an Independent Spirit Award nomination playing a heroin addict in *Requiem for a Dream* (2000) and, a year later, an Oscar for *A Beautiful Mind*, in which she portrayed the real-life physicist wife of schizophrenic mathematician John Nash. With some detours into the Marvelverse (2003's *Hulk*) and ensemble rom-com (*He's Just Not That Into You*, 2009), Connelly continued building a résumé of deeply researched somber roles. So it might surprise some to hear that when she was offered the chance to join the cast of a sequel to *Top Gun*, she jumped at it. "I'm pretty sure I saw it, like almost everyone else, when it came out in the mid-'80s," she says of the original film. "It was exciting, and the soundtrack was a lot of fun, and the flying was just—I'd never seen anything like it before."

Still, she was initially skeptical of what a contemporary follow-up might look like. "It's a film that people love so much. I feel like you don't want to go near a sequel of a film that's so beloved unless there's a really great story to tell," she says. "And I feel like they found a really great story here." But it was the character—Penny Benjamin, the self-sufficient and good-natured owner of a bar near the TOPGUN base—that sold her on the idea. "I loved her optimism," says the actress. "She's incredibly positive and loves to live life to the fullest." Connelly says Penny and Maverick go way back. "Penny's someone that he has known off and on over the years, and there's a romantic connection between them," she teases, refusing to give away any more except that "she's someone that can really go toe-to-toe with him." It isn't exactly a huge spoiler. As director Joseph Kosinski notes, "Of course, you have to have a romantic angle in a *Top Gun* film!"

The new film reunites her with Kosinski and costar Miles Teller, with whom she made the 2017 firefighter drama *Only the Brave*. Incredibly, however, for two stars with such extensive filmographies, she and Cruise had never worked together before now. "Tom has so much positive energy, so much dedication. You can feel it in every moment," she says. "And that carried through every day working with him on the set."

The film also offered her another first: "I had the chance to fly in one of the planes," she says. "It's a World War II plane, very old, very small." The P-51 features just a half dome of glass to enclose the pilot and passenger. In the past, such exposure would've terrified the star. "I went through a patch of having been afraid of flying," she admits. "It lasted a number of years. Fortuitously I had just decided that I needed to be over it. It had nothing to do with the timing of this movie. I just said, 'This is it. I travel too much. I have to outthink this fear that I have.' And I managed to get over it, which was just in time to take this on."

MILES TELLER ★ AS ★ ROOSTER

HIS CHARACTER—THE SON OF MAVERICK'S LATE PAL GOOSE—BRINGS AN EMOTIONAL DEPTH TO THE NEW FILM. OFFSCREEN TELLER BROUGHT LAUGHS TO THE SET

BY ERIK FORREST JACKSON

WITH HIS CASTING in *Top Gun: Maverick,* Miles Teller found himself putting a new spin on an iconic '80s film for the second time in his career. (Impressive for a guy who wasn't born until 1987.) In 2011 he starred in a remake of *Footloose* as Willard, the role Chris Penn had played in the 1984 film. Now he's Bradley "Rooster" Bradshaw, the son of Goose, Maverick's ill-fated best pal played by Anthony Edwards. "[With *Footloose,*] you're playing the exact same character—hopefully interpreting it a little differently—but same character, same story," he says. For *Maverick*, "I'm grateful that I was playing Goose's son. I didn't have to try and play Goose, because Anthony owns that," says Teller. "It was exciting to create my own character, but at the same time figure out where it could be kind of a nod to Goose." He also had a part in selecting his character's call name, Rooster. "I'm sure Anthony Edwards got called Goose way more than he got called Anthony for those next couple of years," says Teller. "So it has to be something you're comfortable with."

It's equally likely that people will stop him on the street to ask if they're related; the two actors look remarkably similar in *Top Gun* and its sequel. To this point Teller was best known for films such as *The Spectacular Now* (2013), for which he and costar Shailene Woodley won a shared Sundance jury prize and his turn as an ambitious jazz drummer in *Whiplash.* Audiences got to see his action side in the first of three installments in the Divergent sci-fi trilogy.

Those films had their fair share of challenging physicality, but *Maverick* took Teller to new extremes. Thanks to a training contraption called the Dunker, devised to prepare pilots for water escapes, he learned that "if I'm ever blindfolded and strapped to a chair upside down underwater, I can get out," he says with pride. To free himself and surface took him about 30 seconds, which felt like forever. Then there was the flying. "I never worried that my life was in danger or anything like that," he says. "Honestly I was too busy trying to act like I'm flying the aircraft to be worried about, 'Oh ... that was pretty close!' That being said, there were a few times in the back of my head I was like, 'Damn, that seemed very close to me.' "

With all the training they endured, the cast more than earned a few lighthearted moments. Once during a long day, Teller secretly brought a mini speaker on-set during a scene with Cruise. "Just before the take, I started playing the 'Top Gun Anthem' from the soundtrack," he says. Everyone cracked up. "It was good to remind ourselves that in the first film, Tom was sitting in the seat we're sitting in."

Cruise had his sweet revenge, though. One day near Christmas, "Tom had set up this whole sweet shop with tons of cookies and cakes. So gracious and thoughtful, but Tom's not eating any of that stuff," says Teller. "He's like, 'Eat up, eat up, Rooster.' And we had a running joke that, because I had to stay in really great shape throughout the whole movie, especially leading up to the beach football scene, he was going to turn Rooster into a turducken."

SECOND GENERATION
"People who lose their parents young, it's amazing as they grow up, seeing how much of that DNA they still have," he says of his character. "The nature vs. nurture thing."

★ THE CLASS OF 2022 ★

YOUNG GUNS

MEET THE NEW STARS PLAYING *TOP GUN: MAVERICK*'S NEW ELITE PILOTS

BY ERIK FORREST JACKSON

LEWIS PULLMAN AS BOB ▸

In a crew of colorful call signs, Lt. Robert Floyd's is Bob. Just Bob. "Yeah, not 'Chainsaw Master Sitting in a Field of Flames,'" he says. "Nothing quite as badass as that." The actor, who won notice in the 2018 thriller *Bad Times at the El Royale*, explains that call signs often grow out of "some massively embarrassing story." But Pullman's character is "quiet, he works hard, and he's sometimes a little socially off. His real name is Bob, and they decided, 'We'll never understand this dude. Let's just call him Bob.'" If his real name and face seem a little familiar, yes, he's the son of actor Bill Pullman, whom Lewis calls "my mentor." But for this role he was flying solo. He recalls asking his dad for advice on juggling *Maverick*'s technical and acting demands. "He was like, 'Listen, man, that's all you. I don't know what to tell you. That's crazy.'"

◂ DANNY RAMIREZ AS FANBOY

Ramirez first watched *Top Gun* when he was a sophomore studying acting at NYU. "I was shook that I hadn't seen it earlier," he recalls. "I thought, 'Where has this been my whole life?'" The Chicago native, who is of Mexican and Colombian heritage and had noteworthy turns in the series *Blindspot* and *The Affair*, says he immediately started "dreaming of a Latinx character in the potential sequel." Sure enough, he managed to score the role of Lt. Mickey Garcia, a weapon-systems operator who goes by the call sign Fanboy. "A pianist has his keys, a painter has his paintbrush, and Fanboy has his instruments in the backseat," says Ramirez. The actor confesses that he signed on to the project while harboring a big secret: When the filmmakers asked if he was afraid of flying, Ramirez fibbed and said no. He had to work through his trepidations with the film's aviation instructors, and he felt buoyed by the other actors cast as pilots as they all endured the vigorous preproduction flight-training program. "By the end of the experience, I was hooked," says Ramirez. "I wanted to keep going back on the Extra 300, which is a small aerobatic monoplane, and the L-39 and F-18 jets." It wasn't all work and no play, however. On days off the tight-knit ensemble kicked back for group movie nights and pool time at their hotel in San Diego. "That's my family right there," says Ramirez. "It's constant banter on the group chats. Theirs are the first texts I wake up to and the last texts I see when I go to sleep."

MONICA BARBARO AS PHOENIX ▸

"I have a very high pain tolerance," says Barbaro, who revved up season 2 of *UnREAL* as stealth villain Yael but came by her toughness through years of ballet. "With dance, in spite of the physical discomfort, there's a commitment to just forging on," she says. "Pulling Gs requires a certain clenching of the body so that you don't pass out." Barbaro dug deep to distinguish herself as Lt. Natasha Trace, the rare female pilot. "The guys recognized my grit and work ethic. I earned their respect on that level, and I think that's what female aviators have to do every day." Living up to her character's call sign, Phoenix, "I rose from the ashes the morning after a big night with the guys in the club. People seemed surprised that I popped up the next day!"

◄ JAY ELLIS AS PAYBACK

"I come from three generations of Air Force," says Ellis, who broke family ranks by going into acting. When he shared the news that he was cast in a *Top Gun* sequel as Lt. Reuben Fitch, his father didn't miss a chance to play up the friendly rivalry between the services. "He was like, 'That's amazing. But that's the Navy, right? Too bad…but at least you're making it.'" In fact, the actor has been making it for a while, in BET's gridiron series *The Game,* HBO's *Insecure* and in the psycho-horror flick *Escape Room*. None of it prepared him for the challenges of *Maverick*. To begin with the actor, who at 6'4" is "at the cutoff for what they allow height-wise," in a fighter jet cockpit. "It's a tight squeeze." But Ellis, a new dad, says, "what I was most concerned about was making sure I nailed my performance so when my daughter sees *Top Gun: Maverick* in a few years, she's like, 'That's my daddy!'"

GLEN POWELL AS HANGMAN ►

"You know when your dad is teaching you to throw a baseball for the first time and you can tell it's like a moment for him?" Powell, who plays Lt. Jake Seresin, laughs at the memory of being 10 and having his father show him *Top Gun* for the first time. "I probably made his hand bleed from doing the *Top Gun* high five with him so many times." Years later, when he got an audition for *Maverick*, Powell left nothing to chance. He tracked down a fighter pilot he'd met at a bachelor party and spent a week and a half at the Miramar base near San Diego immersing himself in that world. "By the time I walked into that audition, I felt there was no possible way that any other actor was going to be more *Top Gun* than me," he says. It worked. During filming he and Tom Cruise bonded over their interest in aviation. As a Christmas gift, Cruise surprised Powell by gifting him real-life pilot training. "It was something I always wanted to do my entire life," he says, "and I got to do it through my hero."

◂ GREG TARZAN DAVIS AS COYOTE

Originally hired for a smaller role, the New Orleans native so impressed the other producers that they expanded his role, Lt. Javy Machado, to include air sequences. That meant, he says, "I had to catch up to the other pilots' training hours." The rest of the cast already had a month of drills, including water evacuation. And Davis didn't know how to swim. He watched YouTube tutorials and practiced at the pool at his L.A. apartment complex, "because you don't want to let Tom down." Fittingly, his character was given the call sign Coyote. "The coyote is the lesser of the other dog packs, but he's fierce and still goes after his prey. He got the name because he had to work hard to prove that he could handle anything that was thrown at him."

GREAT MEMORIES Hamm recalls the 1986 film as "a big topic of conversation amongst the eighth grade boys. You're like, 'Oh my God! You see *Top Gun*? So good!'"

JON HAMM

★ AS ★

CYCLONE

THE ACTOR BRINGS SQUARE-JAWED COMMAND TO A KEY ROLE: THE AUTHORITY FIGURE WHOM MAVERICK RAILS AGAINST. (HE ALSO SHARES WHAT A 'WELCOME ABOARD' HUG FROM TOM CRUISE IS LIKE)

JON HAMM STILL REMEMBERS the chance meeting while at Jimmy Kimmel's house for a Sunday football-watching party. "Jimmy's got, like, 900 TVs, and it was a bunch of dudes, and we'd make pizzas and hang out," says Hamm, who at that time was in the midst of his eight-year run on *Mad Men*, playing the devilishly charming ad exec Don Draper. After years of waiting tables and kicking around L.A. landing small roles, Hamm was finally a star. And yet he didn't quite believe he had joined the kind of circle that would include someone like Tom Cruise, who was in a whole different fame league. "Jimmy said, 'Yeah, Tom Cruise is going to come over,' and we're like, 'Okay, sure. Tom Cruise isn't going to come over. Tom Cruise just doesn't come over to people's houses.'" But then Hamm, who recalls wearing flip-flops, stopped in his tracks. "He showed up with his mom, I think. And we were all like, '*Whoa*. Okay.'"

When the first *Top Gun* film came out, Hamm had watched it in St. Louis, where he grew up. "I must have been 14, which is pretty much bull's-eye, dead center of the demographic it was appealing to," says Hamm. "Everybody wanted to be Tom Cruise and have that jacket and ride that motorcycle and fly those planes, and it was just awesome. And you watch it today, and it's the same thing. It's just a full-on shot of Hollywood adrenaline."

Flash-forward, and Hamm is now cast in the role of Adm. Beau "Cyclone" Simpson in *Maverick*. When he walked on-set, it was the first time he'd seen Cruise since Kimmel's house. Had the star remembered? Maybe, but nonetheless, Cruise greeted Hamm with a big hug. "He's like, 'So happy you're on this. I can't wait. I've been wanting to work with you for so long. It's going to be so great.' Just so positive it's infectious," Hamm says, adding, "When Tom Cruise gives you a hug, man, you've been hugged. It's like a whole thing."

Onscreen, their relationship is less amiable. "I play the air boss—he's the authority figure that Maverick bristles against." Many of his scenes are in uniform, he says, "so I was very aware of my posture and what I'd consumed the night before. We were definitely encouraged to stay fit, for sure."

He reveled in the time he got to spend on Navy vessels docked in San Diego, which he found infinitely cool, if a bit cramped. "Aircraft carriers are not exactly the most comfortable places to be," he says. "There are a lot of hard edges and not a lot of personal space. It's another reminder of how impressive it is what Navy crews go through on a day-to-day basis." He found himself moving around very carefully. "You're walking a little bit like a toddler or a baby deer. You're very, very gingerly going through the motions. I was very pleased that I didn't bang my head or my shin."

Despite the dangers, Hamm found filming *Maverick* to be a series of pinch-me moments. "If I could tell my 14-year-old self, 'Hang in there, man, and one day you might get to work with Tom Cruise,' my 14-year-old self would have been like, 'Yeah, whatever. Okay, boomer.' And then bailed out on me." **—E.F.J.**

ED HARRIS ★ AS ★ HAMMER

ACCLAIMED FOR PLAYING PAINTERS AND POETS, HE'S ALSO DEVELOPED A SPECIALTY IN EMBODYING MILITARY MEN. THE LATEST: MAVERICK'S TOUGH REAR ADM. CHESTER 'HAMMER' CAIN

THE SAME YEAR TOM CRUISE WAS sliding across the floor in his socks in *Risky Business*, Ed Harris was soaring as Marine Corps-flier-turned-astronaut John Glenn in *The Right Stuff*. In the decades since, Harris has proven himself indispensable in a variety of roles—a dying poet (*The Hours*), an artistic genius (*Pollock*, which he also directed) and a godlike reality TV producer in *The Truman Show*. Yet, for some reason, directors love putting him in uniform. "I've played a number of military guys in my life," Harris tells *People*. (Among them: John McCain in HBO's *Game Change* and George Patton in 2020's *Resistance*.) Most of these were "pretty straight, pretty strict and by the numbers." But in his own life, he adds, "I like to go outside the box." Whatever the reason—perhaps because he still wears a crew cut so very well—*Top Gun: Maverick* got the four-time Oscar nominee reenlisted as Rear Adm. Chester "Hammer" Cain.

You won't see him flying. In fact, when he crosses paths with Capt. Pete "Maverick" Mitchell, "he's trying to shut down the testing that they're doing on a supersonic jet," says Harris. "[Cain] just thinks that this particular jet is obsolete—it's not going to be manufactured anymore, so there's no reason to keep testing it." He chuckles. "Maverick feels otherwise."

While Harris stayed earthbound, he calls one very close encounter with a plane "exhilarating." It occurred in a scene where Maverick takes a jet for a test run. Just as Cain arrives at the base's entrance

NOT PLAYING
Onscreen Harris is all business. Between takes? "I usually bring my baseball gloves with me," he says. "I'll find a crew member or actor to have a catch with."

gate, says Harris, "this supersonic jet goes flying about 30 ft. above my head. Well, it was a rush, and it blew the roof off the guard station. They had to fix that, and then they did it again."

Maverick reunites Harris with Cruise, his costar in *The Firm*, and Jerry Bruckheimer, who produced *The Rock* and *National Treasure: Book of Secrets*, in which he appeared. "It was nice working with those guys again," he says. "I had a good time with Tom. We had a good scene in the office there, when he comes in and I try to dress him down. He stands up for himself, of course."

Having worked on-set for just a few days, Harris is looking forward to enjoying *Maverick* as a spectator; at the time of our interview he had yet to see the finished film. "I saw some preliminary footage, and man, I was white-knuckle," he says. "Some of the aerial shots and stuff in these jets is kind of unbelievable."

After filming wrapped, Harris experienced a rush of a different sort, appearing on Broadway as Atticus Finch in *To Kill a Mockingbird*. The run included a history-making filmed performance for 18,000 schoolkids at Madison Square Garden: "That was an experience I won't forget." Next up is *The Ploughman*, the third film he will direct. Something of an elder statesman among the young *Top Gun* actors, Harris recalled a piece of advice he'd been given when he was starting out. "I had a director I worked with in theater before I'd made any kind of films, and he said, 'Ed, stay as far away from Hollywood as possible. Just keep doing your work and getting better and better. They'll come and find you.'" Mission accomplished. **—E.F.J.**

BASHIR SALAHUDDIN ★ AS ★ HONDO

A TV-COMEDY WRITER AND ACTOR, HE HAD ONCE DREAMED OF BEING A PILOT—HE GOT CLOSE

Growing up on the South Side of Chicago, Salahuddin plastered the walls of his bedroom with jet posters. "Fighter pilot was definitely on my short list of totally attainable jobs," he jokes. The dream wasn't entirely far-fetched: His father, an airline mechanic, flew small planes. In his teens Salahuddin saw his aviation ambitions eclipsed by an interest in medicine, and he went on to earn a premed degree from Harvard. Yet another hairpin turn was ahead, though, when he shifted his focus to comedy writing. He spent four years on staff at *Late Night With Jimmy Fallon* while acting on *Superstore, The Mindy Project* and *GLOW*. He also created the shows *South Side* for Comedy Central and *Sherman's Showcase* (IFC). Then, after an impossible run of overachievement, he realized his dream of being a fighter pilot—or at least fighter-pilot adjacent—when he was cast as warrant officer Bernie "Hondo" Coleman, Maverick's friend and a crucial part of the pilots' support team. Before filming began he, along with fellow cast members, visited a real aircraft carrier at sea. They spoke to the crew and ducked under jet exhaust. "A once-in-a-lifetime experience," Salahuddin says. "I felt like a kid at an amusement park."

CHARLES PARNELL ★ AS ★ WARLOCK

WITH PRIOR MILITARY ROLES ON HIS RÉSUMÉ, THE CHICAGO ACTOR BRINGS A VETERAN PRESENCE TO THE *TOP GUN* TEAM

Filming *Maverick* was a mini reunion for Parnell. The actor (and *All My Children* alumnus!) had spent four years working on the TNT action-drama *The Last Ship,* which, like *Maverick,* enjoyed the cooperation of the U.S. Navy. When he turned up on the *Top Gun* sequel set, he encountered some of the same military advisers he had worked with on his earlier gig. "They're there to support you, to make you feel authentic," says Parnell, who plays Adm. Solomon "Warlock" Bates. "In my mind, he's a character from the first movie that you didn't see," he says. Bates and Tom Cruise's Capt. Pete Mitchell "kind of started at the same place. Maverick was Maverick, but Bates went up the chain of command. He's a sage, straight-and-narrow career military guy." He's also an ally to bullheaded Maverick. Off-camera, too, Parnell found an ally in the film's lead actor. "Working with him is like being on a team with a star athlete," he says of Cruise. "But when he gets there, he spends most of his time telling you how great you're doing." He must have meant it—Parnell later landed a part in *Mission Impossible 7* **—E.F.J.**

A FAN FAVE Kilmer (in 2020) has said that leaning on his movie past (as at a 2019 *Top Gun* screening, right) can get him down. But, "it does enable me to meet my fans, and what ends up happening is that I feel really grateful."

VAL KILMER ★ AS ★ ICEMAN

STEPPING BACK INTO HIS *TOP GUN* ROLE FELT 'LIKE BEING REUNITED WITH A LONG-LOST FRIEND,' SAYS THE ACTOR

Can you imagine another actor in the role of the flinty flyboy Tom "Iceman" Kazansky? If Val Kilmer had had his way back in 1985, it would have been anyone but him. Although he was a young, hungry actor with just two film credits (the comedies *Top Secret!* and *Real Genius*), Kilmer had tried hard to stay out of *Top Gun*. "I didn't want the part. I didn't care about the film. The story didn't interest me," the actor wrote in a 2020 memoir, *I'm Your Huckleberry*. "My agent, who also represented Tom Cruise, basically tortured me into at least meeting Tony Scott." Kilmer agreed but did his best to blow his chances at a role. At the audition, he writes, "I showed up looking the fool.... I read the lines indifferently." He got the job and was ultimately won over by the director's enthusiasm, both for his cast and those shiny planes. He made fast friends with many of his costars and was wowed by the finished product, which launched him to a new level of fame. Kilmer moved to the front ranks of American actors, assaying roles as varied as rock gods (Jim Morrison in *The Doors*) to superheroes (*Batman Forever*). In 2013 he crossed paths again with *Top Gun* cohort Anthony Edwards when, in a sly joke, they performed the voices of two fighter jets in *Planes*, Pixar's *Cars* spinoff. Two years later Kilmer's voice was damaged by throat cancer and a subsequent tracheotomy; in 2021, while promoting the documentary *Val*, he announced that he is cancer-free. Unable to speak well, he turned to painting as a creative outlet and shows his work professionally. But when he heard about a potential *Top Gun* sequel, it was the once-reluctant Kilmer doing the hard sell to bring back Iceman. His successful pitch made him the only cast member besides Cruise to reprise his role. His onscreen time is brief but incredibly affecting; it may be among the year's most talked-about movie performances. Kilmer answered *People*'s questions via email. **—E.F.J.**

AMAZON ORIGINAL DOCUMENTARY

VAL

FESTIVAL DE CANNES

THE LIFE YOU LIVE IS THE STORY YOU TELL

BOARDWALK

A24

AMAZON STUDIOS

COMING SOON TO THEATERS

AUG 6 | prime video

KILMER & CO.
For the 2021 biographical documentary *Val*, the actor provided his own video-diary footage from years of having a camcorder on film sets. His son Jack (at right, with Val and sister Mercedes in 2017) read the doc's narration. "My dad's been crazy prolific since he was diagnosed with cancer," Jack Kilmer told *People*.

How was it being back as Iceman?
KILMER It's the strangest thing an actor gets to experience—perhaps once in a lifetime, except those lucky actors blessed with a sequel—because the characters never really go away. They live on in deep freeze, if you'll pardon the pun.

What did you enjoy about it?
Being able to have the characters grow in such surprising and nuanced ways—can't give away more than that, but I promise you it's worth the wait. Myself, I would've waited perhaps a decade instead of two, and I would've let Iceman race Maverick on a Ducati!

What was your relationship with Tom Cruise like then and now?
I am happy to announce we have home movies to prove how much fun we had! Tom Cruise has that rare kind of enthusiasm, as if you've just started your very first film. He is absolutely unmatched in his cheer and joy about the whole process. I think it's why he still hasn't directed a feature yet—he hasn't wrung out every last drop of joy from acting.

How did it feel to reunite with the

old team behind the scenes?
Heaven. I framed a letter [producer] Jerry Bruckheimer wrote me, and I carry one of the gifts Tom gave me in my backpack. Sound corny? You only live once. Unless God blessed you to be an actor, and then you get to live 1,000 lives, and some great parts people love so much they tattoo them to their arms and legs.

What prompted you to write your memoir when you did?
I think it was all the love and enthusiasm foisted on me from social media once I started exploring it as a storytelling medium. Plus, I have to admit, people repeatedly say, "I really like the way you tell a story. Why don't you write a book about all your adventures?" Be it going up in an F-14 or singing show tunes off-key with Marlon Brando till the sun comes up over the Great Barrier Reef or Al Pacino paying me the highest compliment I've ever been paid by an actor besides the one Tom Cruise was kind enough to share with me—but I'm just gonna keep that one to myself. We have to keep some treasures to ourselves so the well don't run dry.

TOM IS MY COPILOT
Cruise and Monica Barbaro talk through a scene. "Tom gave us such a comprehensive training program, we'd be overprepared when the time came to film the thing," she says.

★ THE MAKING OF *MAVERICK* ★

MEET YOUR NEW INSTRUCTOR

THE CREATIVE TEAM REVEAL HOW THEY PULLED OFF NEVER-BEFORE-SEEN AERIAL SEQUENCES. PLUS: TOM CRUISE'S PLAN TO TURN ACTORS INTO FLIERS. SAYS ONE (REAL) NAVY MAN: 'EVERYONE THOUGHT HE WAS CRAZY'

BY ALLISON ADATO

THE CALL CAME IN the middle of the night. Jerry Bruckheimer picked up the phone; it was Tom Cruise, and he sounded concerned. The producer and the actor were working on a sequel to their 1986 hit *Top Gun*, and Cruise was fretting over a particular effect in the new film, which had completed photography and now was being edited for sound. In the more than three decades between *Top Gun* and *Top Gun: Maverick*, both military flight and moviemaking technology had evolved significantly. So what was on the star's mind at this late hour? Bruckheimer recalls: "Tom says, 'You know that door closing in Cain's office? It's too loud. We should fix it.'"

It's been 36 years since Pete "Maverick" Mitchell first felt the need for speed. *Top Gun* topped the box office in its day and set its star on a path to an action-movie career of unprecedented scope. Faced with making a sequel so long-anticipated, Cruise could be forgiven for wanting every element—down to the *click* of a door in its frame—to be exactly right. "There's no detail that escapes his eyes, his ears or his brain," says Bruckheimer. "He wants optimum in everything."

Most of all, he wanted optimum flying. Cruise, who became a licensed pilot after making *Top Gun*, thought the aerial sequences in *Maverick* should be unlike any in movies before. He intended to far exceed what the first film achieved when the actors filmed their close-ups in cutaway cockpits on a soundstage in Burbank. In other words: He wanted to do the flying for real.

"Everybody thought he was crazy," says Capt. Brian "Ferg" Ferguson, the sequel's Navy aerial adviser. Actors would have to deliver in-flight performances without blacking out from extreme acceleration. Pilots would need to execute the challenging missions—choreographed dogfights or high-speed passes through rocky canyons—that give the movie its thrills, while bearing in mind plot and cinematography. And filmmakers would need to rig a slew of cameras inside the Navy's $67.4 million F-18 Super Hornet fighter jets to capture it all.

"Tom said it wasn't worth doing unless we were going to do it real: in the airplane, flying the pilots to their limits." To Ferguson's mind, "it probably would have looked almost as good if you would have done it using [special effects] technology." In fact, the

ANY QUESTIONS?
Above: Cruise reviewing footage of Barbaro with the cast. "I'll have them look at it—what's working, what's not," he says. She rode with CDR Kristen "Dragon" Hansen, one of two female pilots among the real flight crew.

READY TO ROLL
Left: Six IMAX cameras captured each cockpit scene. They had to be mounted in the F-18s so that "if the pilot and the passenger had to eject, the camera system didn't interfere," says director Kosinski. He designed the rig, which took a year to win approval from the Navy.

BETWEEN TAKES
"We put him through hell with the flying," says Jerry Bruckheimer of Miles Teller (right, with the producer, on-set). "There's a side of him, a wonderful sense of humor, he's only showed it in a few movies. You can see the fun he has."

comparatively low-tech 1986 film had so inspired him as a teen, he says it was one reason he joined the Navy.

Call it the *Top Gun* effect. Maybe every critic didn't love the movie—"the good parts are so good and the bad parts are so relentless," lamented Roger Ebert back then—but for certain viewers, it was life-changing; Navy recruitment spiked following its release. If detractors charged that it glorified combat, fans were transfixed by the spectacular feats of flight. Plus, aviators were *cool*, down to their namesake sunglasses.

David Ellison saw the movie at 8 years old, when his father showed it to him at home on LaserDisc. "It just blew me away, and I said, 'I want to be able to do that one day.' I started flying when I was 13. I used to do competitive aerobatics and fly air shows." Joseph Kosinski was 11 when he and some friends saw it at the Orpheum in Marshalltown, Iowa. "I desperately

"WHEN I WAS A KID, THEY HAD THIS RIDE CALLED THE GRAVITRON. IT WOULD SPIN IN CIRCLES. I DON'T KNOW HOW MANY Gs THAT THING IS, BUT DEFINITELY TIMES THAT BY A COUPLE"

—MILES TELLER, ON FLYING IN A NAVY JET

wanted to be a pilot, because of the incredible footage," Kosinski recalls. Instead he grew up to earn degrees in mechanical engineering and architecture. But because this is a Hollywood story, he then moved to Los Angeles and wrote a treatment for what became the 2013 sci-fi action flick *Oblivion,* starring Tom Cruise. Ellison, meanwhile, became a producer; his company Skydance Media has partnered with Cruise to produce eight films, including five in the *Mission Impossible* franchise (the last two are slated for release in 2023 and 2024).

Kosinski put himself forward to direct *Top Gun*'s next chapter with a three-pronged pitch: "What would be the most exciting way to find Maverick today? Second, how can we engage the audience in the most emotional way? Third, how can we capture what it looks and feels like to be in an F-18 Super Hornet?" says Kosinski, who—spoiler—got the gig.

The story picks up with Capt. Pete "Maverick" Mitchell three decades after his graduation from the TOPGUN program. Others of his generation have moved up the ranks; Mitchell is now a fiftysomething test pilot, albeit one whose outsize skill and taste for risky maneuvers make him uniquely qualified to head up the training for a dangerous new mission. "He's called back to TOPGUN," says Kosinski. But now Maverick is the instructor, not the bratty student. Among his young charges is Lt. Bradley "Rooster" Bradshaw, the son of his best friend, Lt. Nick "Goose" Bradshaw (Anthony Edwards in the first movie), who was killed when they ejected together from a plane. Maverick's bond with Rooster, played by Miles Teller, is the "emotional spine of the story," says Kosinski. "That was the thing that really got Tom engaged."

There would also be a love story. Jennifer Connelly took the role of Penny Benjamin, a single mom who shares a past with Maverick. (*Top Gun* superfans will recall her name from a moment when Maverick is said to have "a history of high-speed passes over five air-control towers and *one admiral's daughter*.") "I always wanted to work with her; she can do anything," says Cruise of Connelly, adding that her ad-libs helped flesh out the character, who now runs a bar near the Navy base. Naturally there's a bar because you need a

> IT MAKES YOU FEEL VERY SAFE TO BE IN THE HANDS OF SOMEONE LIKE THAT. BECAUSE IF HE SAYS, 'TRUST ME ON THIS,' YOU KNOW HE'S GOOD FOR IT"
>
> **—GLEN POWELL ('HANGMAN'), ON CRUISE**

place for the inevitable singing—it wouldn't be a *Top Gun* movie without it. Says Connelly: "When I talk about the fact that we've been making this sequel, it's overwhelming how nostalgic people feel."

Where touchstone reboots often rely on getting the whole gang back together, the only other *Top Gun* alumnus is Val Kilmer, reprising the role of Iceman. "The rivalry between Iceman and Maverick was such a memorable part of the first movie," says Kosinski. "I'm glad we'll be able to show the evolution of that relationship." Beyond that, *Maverick* leans into new characters, some played by veterans like Ed Harris and Jon Hamm, though there is also a crop of fresh names in the roles of the pilot trainees. (See page 28.)

Most of these performers hadn't even been born when *Top Gun* premiered, yet all understood what appearing in its sequel could mean for their careers. What they did not know, at least not initially, was the plan to film them in jets going more than 500 mph. They began to get a hint during casting.

"We would ask them, 'Do you get sick on roller coasters? Do you have a fear of flying?'" says executive producer Tommy Harper. "We wanted to make sure they knew it was not just that they couldn't throw up, they actually had to *act*." Cruise went further: "I was very clear in the beginning: 'This is what it's going to be like. It's not for everyone,'" he says. "I want people to enjoy the experience. 'If you don't want be involved totally, I understand.'" At least one, Danny Ramirez, exaggerated his comfort level. "You had to sign a paper basically saying you weren't [afraid to fly], and I was like, 'Well, I'm definitely terrified of being in the air, but I can't pass up on this.'" He won the part of Fanboy, becoming one of seven new cast members who would fly under conditions otherwise experienced only by actual military aviators. "When you shoot it real, it just feels different," says producer Ellison. "You can't fake the Gs on the actor's face."

The Gs. Meaning, the gravitational force from acceleration. If you've forgotten your high school physics, here's a refresher: 1G is the pull that keeps us from floating off Earth. A roller coaster might expose you to 3 or 4 Gs, that feeling of being pressed into the seat. The extreme climbs, dives and accelerations of a fighter jet can create 8 or 9 Gs—enough to make a person black out

GROUND CREW
"I work with people that I respect, so I want to hear their opinion," says Cruise (with director Kosinski, left, in gray, and cast members).

from the blood rushing from their heads; some of the actors nearly did. Specialized flight suits can help withstand such pressure, and practice does too—professional pilots learn to get used to G forces by logging time in the air. So that's what the new cast would do.

But first, safety. Even being a passenger in an F-18 meant extensive required Navy training. Says Kosinski: "It was a boot-camp mentality. Nothing brings people together like group suffering." They had to learn how to pound their way out of a cockpit. Swim 150 meters in full flight gear. Perform underwater drills should they be forced to eject over the ocean. "That involves being strapped into this dunker, and you have to trust your buddy to open a window in time and swim out and holding your breath and upside-down, disoriented," reports Monica Barbaro (Phoenix). "Overcoming my fears during the swim phase was something that probably changed me for life."

Back in the mid-'80s, Cruise had undergone safety prep but had nothing to otherwise ready him for his job in *Top Gun*. "I just got in the F-14, talked about story, and then it went." The actors in his charge would have a different ride. "Tom set up the exact course that he wished he had on the first one," says Lewis Pullman,

> "WE'RE TRYING TO TELL A GOOD STORY. HOW CAN WE GIVE THE AUDIENCE WHAT THEY ENJOY BUT NOT A COVER? WE'RE MAKING AN ORIGINAL FILM"
> **—TOM CRUISE**

who plays Bob. "He knew it's not going to happen unless we have at least two months doing consistent flights." In that time, says Cruise, "I had to teach them how to first fly in a single engine Cessna, to learn the vernacular—it's a whole different verbiage. Then I put them in an airplane where they could do some aerobatics. Then a jet—not an F-18 yet—where they could pull serious Gs and feel what it's like with an ejector seat. The first day they're in the F-18, they're filming."

"My first flight was probably the most terrifying, in a little Cessna," says actor Jay Ellis (Payback), who went up with Glen Powell (Hangman). "Our flight instructor was like, 'Okay, you take over.' I was like, 'You want me to fly the plane? We're like 20,000 ft. [up].' I look over, and Glen is like, 'Don't look at me! Fly the plane, man.' That was the most anxiety I had the entire time. From there, you realize, 'Oh, I got this, this was great.' You're taking off, you're landing. Then we graduated to other planes."

Not everyone took to the high-velocity experience that came next. Three weeks in, Pullman had not acclimated to G forces. "I remember thinking, 'I'm going to be fired. This is grueling. I can't imagine getting through a 50-second scene without puking.'" But he kept at it, aiming for the two-month mark that Cruise had predicted would make the difference. "One of the most thrilling experiences was six weeks in, realizing 'I can do this!' Something I thought was out of the realm of possibility, all of a sudden became not only possible but was incredibly empowering."

To be clear: Nobody is putting civilians at the controls of a Navy jet. (Not even Cruise, who operates his own vintage P-51 prop plane in one of the film's more serene moments.) But the actors still needed to appear as if they were in command. "Pulling Gs is not comfortable," says Barbaro. "To do that while focusing on character is not easy."

WINGMEN, REVISITED
Cruise filming a scene in which Maverick confronts his past.

There was a lot to remember. "The pilot is in the front seat; we're in the back," explains Miles Teller. "If the pilot pulls this stick left and then I pull the stick left even a half a second after that, that's not going to look right. The plane's moving before I'm moving. So you really need to get in sync with your pilot." Cruise's solution? "I built a wooden mock-up of the F-18, where the pilot was sitting in one place and the actor in the other. I had them work together."

Filming took 18 months with each aerial sequence as carefully plotted as it was ambitious. "We went to the great lengths to find the wildest, most visual terrain as you could possibly imagine, the most dynamic aircraft moves we can put on-camera," says aerial coordinator Kevin LaRosa. "The dogfight scenes, the

WHY SO LONG FOR A SEQUEL?

A FEW FALSE STARTS, AND A REAL-LIFE TRAGEDY KEPT FILMMAKERS FROM GIVING FANS A FOLLOW-UP TO THE TOP-GROSSING MOVIE OF 1986

The span from *Top Gun* to *Maverick* isn't the longest between a film and its sequel—*Mary Poppins* holds that distinction, with 54 years before her return. But *Maverick* does boast a notable gap. Why so long? "Don [Simpson] and I tried to develop some stuff right after *Top Gun*. Tom tried to…but we just never cracked it," says Jerry Bruckheimer. (Simpson, who died in 1996, had been his longtime producing partner.) "Then it went dormant." Years later producer and aviation fan David Ellison, a man not much older than *Top Gun* itself, came aboard. He would go on to work with Cruise on the *Mission Impossible* and *Jack Reacher* series, but when he signed a deal with Paramount, recalls Ellison, "the first movie we said we wanted to make was a sequel to *Top Gun*." By 2012 the team, again including director Tony Scott, was back at the TOPGUN school making plans. "Tom and I were there with Tony on a Friday. Tony was really excited about it, interviewing all the pilots," says Bruckheimer. "Then we lost him that Sunday." Scott had died by suicide. (See "Remembering Tony Scott," page 86.) Without him the filmmakers struggled to continue: "There was no force behind it." A new director, Joseph Kosinski, provided that momentum. "Joe came up with the idea, and Tom got really excited based on that pitch," adds Bruckheimer. Originally scheduled for a summer 2020 release, the film got scuttled by the pandemic. But now *Maverick* finally comes in for a landing.

low-level, air-to-ground attack scenes—we're really out there with two or three aircraft and a camera jet or helicopter capturing these."

"There will be speculation that, 'Well, there's no way an actor was in that airplane at 50 ft., inverted, going over the ridge at 580 mph at seven Gs.' But there was!" says Captain Ferguson. While he thought initially they might be wiser to go with special effects, he is now quick to confirm: "Every time you see an actor in an airplane, there is an actor in an airplane." (That's true. There is also a smidgen of CGI. "The only time we use visual effects are maneuvers that we felt had a safety consideration," says Kosinski.)

Meanwhile, even as he was working with the cast on fly-acting, Cruise was helping the real pilots understand that, although they are never on-camera, they, too, were giving a performance. "I take them through the story so that they can get the jet to behave a particular way," he explains. "I had to teach them about cinematography—where the light was, why we needed

THE WRITE STUFF
Above: Cruise with frequent collaborator Christopher McQuarrie, who wrote *Maverick's* screenplay with Ehren Kruger and Eric Warren Singer. Left: Danny Ramirez, Glen Powell, Monica Barbaro, Kosinski (with laptop) and Lewis Pullman share a laugh on-set.

that light. Here's the moment that we're going for. Here's the lines." Ideally he would have assigned one pilot per actor, so each pair could have contributed to a single portrayal. That wasn't possible—the officers have day jobs that don't involve moviemaking. "These guys are the best pilots in the world," says Cruise. "We're working within their maneuvers."

That's the thing about flying in actual Navy planes: You're dealing with the actual Navy. "We were not going to let the film impact any of our real-world operations or training," says CDR Christopher "Pops" Papaioanu, the Naval Aviation technical adviser on the film. He hoped for an accurate depiction of not only dogfights but of the culture at TOPGUN, of which he was commanding officer. "There's no competition between fighter pilots, which was a big staple of the first film. There's no trophy at the end of the class," notes Commander Papaioanu, who read and offered input on the new script. "Probably my biggest concern was how Hollywood typically portrays fighter pilots: as cocky. Certainly we are highly confident people, but it's based on the experience that we have. We don't over-talk ourselves. To a large degree this film got it right."

By the time shooting was done, the cast had earned the respect of the Navy advisers. "I wish I had a good story for you, where maybe they struggled. But they just rocked it," says Commander Papaioanu. "Tom put together a very effective syllabus."

Will the actors ever need this information again, how to eject from a jet or swim in flight gear? Perhaps if there's another sequel in less than 30 years. But the most valuable lessons Cruise offered may have had little to do with planes. "There were times after we were wrapped for the day, we would spend an hour circled around him, listening to the stories that he's been through," says Greg Tarzan Davis, who plays Coyote. It was more than mere tips on acting or navigating the industry. "Every one of the pilots has a story of him talking about what he thinks is great about them, what they can do with that quality," recalls Pullman. "He teaches you, basically, how Tom Cruise became Tom Cruise." **—WITH REPORTING BY EILEEN FINAN AND ERIK FORREST JACKSON**

"A LOT OF STUFF WE'RE DOING, HASN'T BEEN DONE BEFORE. THEY NEVER SHOT PLANES LIKE THIS"
—TOM CRUISE

FRIENDLY SKIES
Barbaro's and Teller's characters "are incredibly good friends," she says. Some of the film's look is a subtle tribute to the first film's director. "We were trying to stay in the vein of Tony Scott," says executive producer Harper, "the textures he did. We always wanted to shoot magic hour."

AT WORK
"What I want to do is give the audience an experience," says Zimmer (above and right, with Harold Faltermeyer).

★ THE MUSIC ★

MAVERICK'S HIGH NOTES

FOR HIS NEW TAKE ON THE ORIGINAL *TOP GUN* SCORE, COMPOSER HANS ZIMMER GOT IN A PLANE. THEN JUMPED.

BY RICHARD JEROME

To create a score for *Maverick*, the Academy Award-winning composer Hans Zimmer could have stayed safely at the keyboard and behind the conductor's podium. Instead he did a kind of musician's version of Method acting: He jumped out of a plane. "I was strapped to an instructor and shoved out of an airplane for free fall, which is a different way of embracing what you're composing," says Zimmer.

Over the past 38 years, Zimmer has scored some 150 movies, capturing his Oscar for 1994's *The Lion King*. His powerfully evocative soundscapes, with rich orchestrations and frequent use of electronics, have also enhanced *Gladiator*, the *Pirates of the Caribbean* series, the *Dark Knight* trilogy, *Inception*, *Dunkirk* and *Blade Runner 2049*. But *Maverick* was no ordinary commission. It would not be a wholly new work but one that built upon themes in the original *Top Gun* score by his pal Harold Faltermeyer—the two hail from the same Munich neighborhood. This would be a labor of love, a way to honor old friends.

The late Tony Scott, who directed *Top Gun*, had offered Zimmer his first scoring job. It fell through, though, and he wound up writing for Barry Levinson's 1988 film *Rain Man*, which began his long professional association with Tom Cruise. "I wanted to be the servant of the memory of what Tony had done and to help Harold, because that is amazing, iconic music," he says. "So I forgot about being the composer—it was more about seeing how I could support Harold's tunes and the other tunes." (Among them: "Danger Zone," performed by Kenny Loggins; for more, see page 92.)

The adrenaline-pumping *Top Gun* score is quintessentially '80s, but Zimmer doesn't see *Maverick*'s music as a 21st-century reboot. "I wanted to be respectful of the heritage of the first movie, without pandering. It was very important for us to give the audience a thrilling new experience while drawing on the earlier material."

When scoring *Maverick*—or any film—Zimmer doesn't get caught up in individual scenes—rather he strives to grasp the soul of the film. "The only way you can do that in an honest way is if the music acts like doors opening. I'm inviting you in to come and feel what this movie is about—to use the language of music to do all those things you can't elegantly say in words or pictures." That's how he found himself strapped into a parachute, trying to get into the mind of characters whose adventures would unfold to his music. "*Maverick*'s a movie which is so visceral," he adds. "A lot of this comes from Tom. I sit him down and make him tell me what this love of flying is all about—because at the end of the day I have one mission only: I want you to come away with an understanding of the love and thrill of flying."

★ LOOK BACK ★

TOP GUN

IN THE SUMMER OF 1986 AN AMBITIOUS MOVIE ABOUT NAVY FLIERS SOARED AT THE BOX OFFICE (AND ON THE RADIO), LAUNCHING THE CAREER OF ITS YOUNG STAR, TOM CRUISE, INTO THE STRATOSPHERE

ALL SYSTEMS GO Cruise (in his original spin as Maverick) was ready for new heights.

★ MAKING *TOP GUN*, 1986 ★

HOW IT TOOK FLIGHT

'*STAR WARS* ON EARTH' PROVED AN IRRESISTIBLE FILM PITCH. BUT GETTING *TOP GUN* TO THE SCREEN WAS A WHOLE OTHER STORY

BY CHRIS NASHAWATY

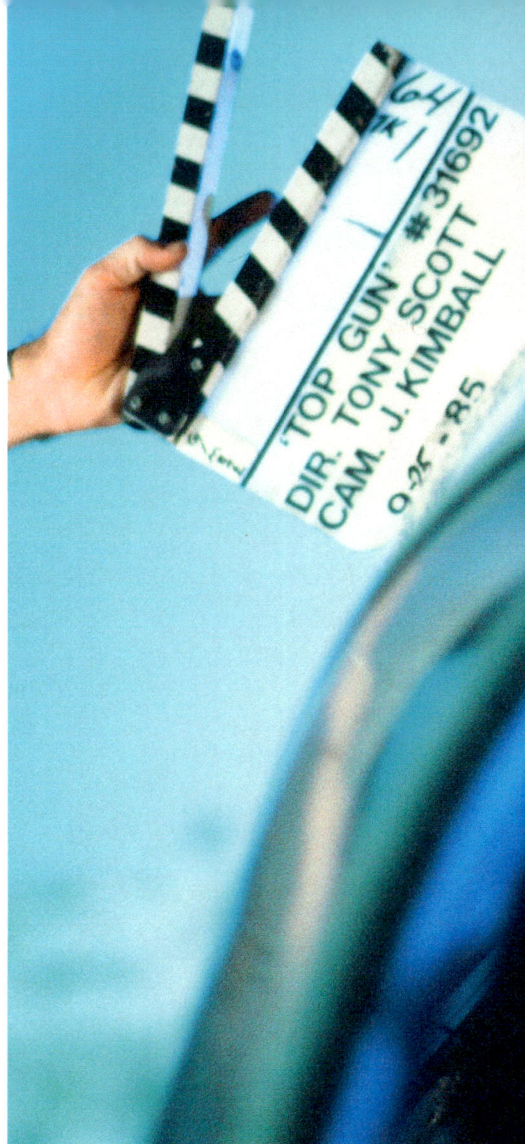

AT MACH 2 AND 40,000 FT. over California, it's always high noon."

The opening sentence of the article in the May 1983 issue of *California* magazine sounded like a hit movie to Jerry Bruckheimer. Written by Israeli journalist Ehud Yonay, the story titled "Top Guns" chronicled the lives of elite young pilots enrolled at the U.S. Navy Fighter Weapons School at Miramar Naval Air Station near San Diego. The slick photographs of uniformed daredevils in F-14s that ran with the piece sealed the deal in the producer's mind.

Along with his coproducer, Don Simpson, Bruckheimer went to Paramount with the idea. Their last film, *Flashdance*, had just opened big for the studio. And their next, *Beverly Hills Cop*, was about to hit even bigger. Bruckheimer boiled his pitch down to four words: "*Star Wars* on Earth."

Somehow the studio honchos didn't see it—at least, not right away. Still, they trusted Simpson and Bruckheimer's track record and gave them a green light to buy the rights to the article and to hire a screenwriter. In the summer of 1983, Jim Cash and Jack Epps Jr. were adapting the comic strip *Dick Tracy* for the screen when they met with Paramount's head of production, Jeffrey Katzenberg, over breakfast to discuss their next project. "He threw out about eight different ideas," recalls Epps. "One of them was this article that Jerry Bruckheimer had found." Cash hated to fly, but Epps had a pilot's license and was obsessed with aviation. He was sold, but still, one concern nagged at him: "If we don't get the planes, we can't do this movie."

IN THE PILOT'S SEAT
Cruise (left) and Kilmer (below) prepare to shoot cockpit scenes. "Tom's love for flying was so real even back then," says Kilmer. "It's endured to this day."

REAL TOMCATS
In addition to providing pilots and technical advisers, the Navy lent the *Top Gun* filmmakers two aircraft carriers and a fleet of F-14 Tomcat jets (below left), charging them only for the planes' fuel: $7,600 per hour in the air.

"TOM AND I WENT TO WASHINGTON AND MET WITH THE SECRETARY OF THE NAVY, [WHO] SAID, 'LOOK, TOM, I LOVE THIS.... YOU'LL GET OUR FULL SUPPORT.'"
—JERRY BRUCKHEIMER, PRODUCER

While it's now become routine for the military to cooperate with Hollywood, it was almost unheard of in the '80s. Undeterred, Bruckheimer got a meeting with the then-Secretary of the Navy, John Lehman, a Reagan appointee who was keen to rebuild the stockpile of warships depleted after the Vietnam War. He also happened to be a cousin of film star Grace Kelly, who had died the previous year. Did that influence his decision? Impossible to say, but Bruckheimer came away with a deal. The filmmakers would give the Navy script approval and pay $1.8 million for the use of its base, planes and aircraft carriers. Former TOPGUN instructor Rear Adm. (ret.) Pete Pettigrew then came on as a technical adviser. Epps packed his bags and headed to Miramar.

Yonay's article had provided an incredible setting but not much of a plot. The screenwriter hung out with pilots and even went up in an F-5 to ride shotgun in a combat training mission. "As a writer, you're always looking for conflict," says Epps. "But these guys were all about teamwork. Then I had that moment where you get hit by lightning: 'One of them is not a team player, he's out for himself.' And that was Maverick." When the writers handed in their finished script, Epps told the producers, "Think Tom Cruise..."

Actually, they already were. But Cruise, who had rocketed to stardom in *Risky Business* and had recently shot the Ridley Scott fantasy *Legend*, wasn't easily wooed. "Tom was always our first choice," says Bruckheimer. "We sent him the script, and he was, at least from our point of view, never committed to it." But after Ridley's brother Tony Scott was brought on as the director of *Top Gun*, Cruise got a nudge. Said Cruise: "Ridley said, 'You've got to meet my brother; he's going to direct this film *Top Gun*...'"

To close the deal, Bruckheimer arranged for Cruise to fly with the Blue Angels. "He'd just finished [*Legend*], and he had a long ponytail," says Bruckheimer. "These pilots take a look at him and say, 'We're gonna give this hippie the ride of his life,' not knowing that

NOT-SO-LONE RIDER
Cruise had learned to handle a Kawasaki GPZ900R motorcycle just before shooting *Top Gun* (above, with the camera crew that accompanied his ride). He's since performed stunts on them in the *Mission Impossible* films. Left: Producer Bruckheimer with Cruise on-set.

"YOU'VE LOST THAT LOVIN' FEELIN'/ WHOA, THAT LOVIN' FEELIN'/ YOU'VE LOST THAT LOVIN' FEELIN'/ NOW IT'S GONE, GONE, GONE, WHOA..."
—THE RIGHTEOUS BROTHERS

WHERE TO GET THAT LOVIN' FEELIN'
Still open, the San Diego restaurant Kansas City Barbeque (founded by two KC natives) saw Maverick sing to Charlie.

TOP GUN'S REAL LOVE STORIES

Meg Ryan, who played Goose's wife, Carole, had just 10 days of shooting with onscreen husband Anthony Edwards. But by the time *Top Gun* was in theaters, he was revealing that their first meeting was "*something* at first sight" and that they had swapped phone numbers. When Edwards finished filming that summer, "I called Meg," he told *People* in 1986, "and we got together in September." Added Ryan: "It's just been one big date ever since." (Adorable, but they didn't last; she met future husband Dennis Quaid on the 1987 film *Innerspace*.) Meanwhile Kelly McGillis and Barry Tubb, who played flyer Henry "Wolfman" Ruth, got close during filming and moved in together afterward. By 1987 they were on-again, off-again, with Tubb telling *People*, "We can't live together and we can't live apart. Kelly is always neat, and I'm messy."

Tom would love that." By the time he set foot back on terra firma, Cruise, a known adrenaline junkie, was in—but for a price. Recalls casting director Margery Simkin: "One day Don Simpson called saying, 'Tom's agent wants $1 million! Who else is there?' There were a lot of great people at the time, like Sean Penn, but they weren't this guy. So I said, 'Pay him!'"

With its $15 million budget—a large chunk of which had already been earmarked for Cruise and the Navy—Simkin was now tasked with recruiting actors to round out the cast: Anthony Edwards became Maverick's partner Goose, Rick Rossovich was

ONSCREEN LOVE
The romance between Cruise and McGillis's characters was initially deemed too cool by test audiences. Scott reshot to turn up the heat.

Slider, John Stockwell became Cougar, rodeo rider Barry Tubb was Wolfman, Tim Robbins became Merlin, and Tom Skerritt was the crusty-but-sympathetic Top Gun instructor. As for the potentially star-making romantic lead of Charlie, *Witness's* Kelly McGillis beat out a relatively unknown Meg Ryan. But Ryan had made such a strong impression in her audition that when a revised version of the script added the part of Goose's wife, she was hired over Holly Hunter. Last but not least was the part of Maverick's nemesis Iceman. Everyone wanted Val Kilmer, but the actor didn't want to do the film. In the end, he was forced to as part of a studio-contract obligation. (He has long ago admitted that making *Top Gun* was a joy, not least because of the cast: "We all laughed till we fell down the hot spiked crabgrass at the Holiday Inn in San Diego," Kilmer tells *People*.)

But the chemistry of the young actors wouldn't become apparent until they reported for duty at Miramar in the summer of 1985. There was all of the partying one would expect from a group of young actors on location, including a run-in with the San Diego police when they packed into a car with Kilmer behind the wheel. There were also a pair of simmering offscreen romances

GREAT SCOTT
"Tony would sketch out each shot that you had to do that day," remembers Skerritt. "You begin to see, 'This is a master, this guy.'"

"MY MAIN JOY WAS THE CAMARADERIE OF THE CAST . . . ALONG WITH THE INCREDIBLE, UNFLAPPABLE ENTHUSIASM OF TONY SCOTT AND TOM CRUISE"
—VAL KILMER

AUTHORITY FIGURE
To prep for his role as "Viper," Skerritt (seated) met with the head of the real TOPGUN academy. "He was quiet, very direct. So I took that on."

I MET TOM [CRUISE] AND SAID, 'YOU'RE REALLY QUITE A GOOD ACTOR. HOW DO YOU COME BY ALL OF THAT?' AND HE SAID THE NICEST THING: 'WELL, I JUST WATCH A GUY LIKE YOU WORK' "
—TOM SKERRITT

THE REAL *TOP GUN* ROLE MODELS

BESIDES SECURING NAVY COOPERATION, FILMMAKERS TURNED TO REAL FLYERS AND INSTRUCTORS FOR BOTH VERACITY AND INSPIRATION

PETE PETTIGREW

Hawk-eyed *Top Gun* fans will recognize Pete Pettigrew as the guy on Kelly McGillis's arm when she walks into the bar where she's serenaded by Tom Cruise. But Pettigrew is no ordinary Hollywood extra. In fact, the retired Navy rear admiral is a decorated Vietnam veteran with more than 325 combat missions. As a technical adviser on the film, he made sure the details were as real as possible, down to the pilots' nicknames. The name he had used in real life, Viper, was given to Tom Skerritt's character. "Although you get a little older, and sometimes they change your call sign," he tells *People*. "Now they tend to call me Diaper." In 1969 Pettigrew became one of the earliest instructors at the U.S. Navy Fighter Weapons School in Miramar, aka TOPGUN. In 1984 Hollywood came calling. After meeting with Cruise and the filmmakers, Pettigrew was on hand to answer endless questions from the screenwriters and advocated to make sure that what appeared onscreen was accurate. "We fought all the time," he says. "I knew that if it wasn't somewhat real, all my fighter-pilot buddies were going to laugh at me. On the other hand, I knew that if it was a documentary, nobody'd go see the movie."

CHRISTINE FOX

If the idea of a young female instructor lecturing a roomful of macho, testosterone-fueled fighter pilots seems like something that could only happen in a Hollywood movie, well, guess again. Years before she became an acting Deputy Secretary of Defense in the Obama Administration in 2013, Christine Fox was a civilian defense analyst working at TOPGUN—and the inspiration for Kelly McGillis's character Charlie. For nearly three decades, the 6-ft. Maryland native and expert in maritime-air superiority worked for the Center for Naval Analyses (CNA), a Navy think tank. Back then she had a sign over the government-issue metal desk in her office that listed the differences between an ape and a fighter pilot. (No. 26: It doesn't take a million dollars to train an ape.) Despite her sense of humor, Fox was serious when she told *People* in a 1985 interview that the similarities between her and Charlie were few and far between. "The fact that I know so much about what these guys are doing every day and they come back in and talk to me about it—why is my radar doing this?—changes the relationship. It takes some of the romance out."

IN TRIBUTE | ART SCHOLL

On the afternoon of Sept. 16, 1985, veteran stunt flyer Art Scholl went up in a Pitts S-2 camera plane to shoot second-unit footage for one of *Top Gun*'s aerial sequences. He'd already gotten the shot, but the consummate perfectionist wanted to try for one more run. Scholl, 53, went into a planned spin, but his plane failed to recover and crashed into the Pacific Ocean. *Top Gun* was dedicated to the memory of Scholl, a married father of two.

YES, THAT'S TIM ROBBINS
"He had this agent who would call me almost every day saying, 'Don't you have a part for Tim?'" recalls casting director Margery Simkin. Soon after *Top Gun*, he landed *Bull Durham*.

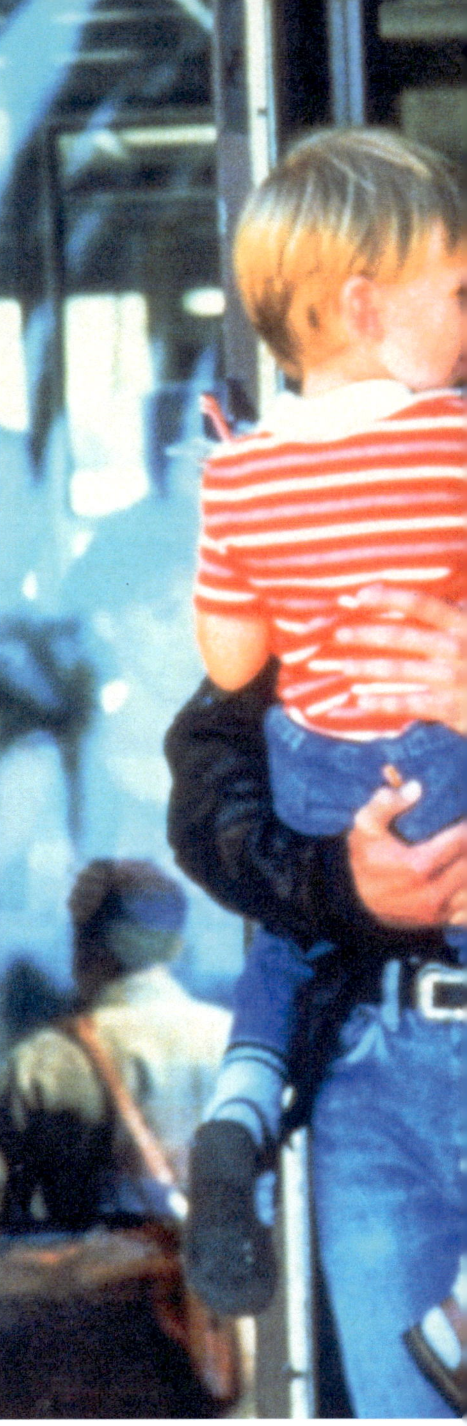

between McGillis and Tubb as well as Edwards and Ryan. But Cruise, whose concentration even at 23 was laser-focused, kept his distance. "We rarely saw Tom," says Kilmer. "He was in virtually every scene, and when he wasn't rehearsing, he was practicing flying or volleyball or singing or riding his motorcycle or a dozen other details." Adds Rossovich: "I knew that Tom's star was going to ascend even back then, because I saw how hard he worked. He was a different animal."

If the nights were a blur, the days were all work. The male actors underwent a grueling training regimen teaching them how to eject from a fighter plane, how to escape from the cockpit underwater and how to deliver their lines while fighting G-forces and hypoxia at 40,000 ft. Only then were they ready to go up in an actual F-14. With the help of some Hollywood trickery, it may look like the actors are flying in the film, but they're actually being flown by a Navy pilot sitting in front. However, says Pettigrew, "they all threw up."

As the Navy's eyes and ears, Pettigrew had to choose his battles trying to balance fact with Hollywood fiction. No, in real life there wasn't a locker room where pilots would trade verbal barbs while wearing towels around their waists. No, civilian instructors didn't wear seamed stockings on the base. He changed what he could but understood they weren't making a documentary. Tragically, however, reality intervened with a reminder that flying is never without some risk, even

LITTLE 'ROOSTER'
The son of Goose (Anthony Edwards) and Carole (Meg Ryan) was played by Adam and Aaron Weis, 4-year-old twins from San Diego.

with all safety precautions taken. Just weeks before filming finished, one of the stunt pilots, Art Scholl, was flying a propeller plane while shooting second-unit material. The 53-year-old crashed in the water.

The accident was still fresh in everyone's mind when *Top Gun* wrapped in the fall of 1985. After months of postproduction, Simpson and Bruckheimer were ready to share the film with a test audience. Their chief complaint was that the romance between Cruise and McGillis needed more spice. So the two actors were called back to shoot new scenes. McGillis had already cut her hair for her next film role, which is why she wears a military cap in her flirt-heavy elevator scene with Cruise. Scott solved the hair problem in their steamy love scene by filming it in silhouette.

Top Gun finally hit theaters on May 16, 1986. It opened at No. 1 with $8.1 million. At the time, the critics were mixed. While some groused about the film's patriotic, Reagan-era politics, almost all praised its thrilling aerial sequences, not to mention the now-undeniable star power of Cruise. Audiences meanwhile made *Top Gun* the highest-grossing movie of 1986 with $356 million at the worldwide box office. But *Top Gun* was never meant to be a critics' movie. It was exactly what Bruckheimer knew it would be when he first saw that *California* magazine article three years earlier: a movie about heroism, bravery, romance, popcorn escapism and the need . . . the need for speed.

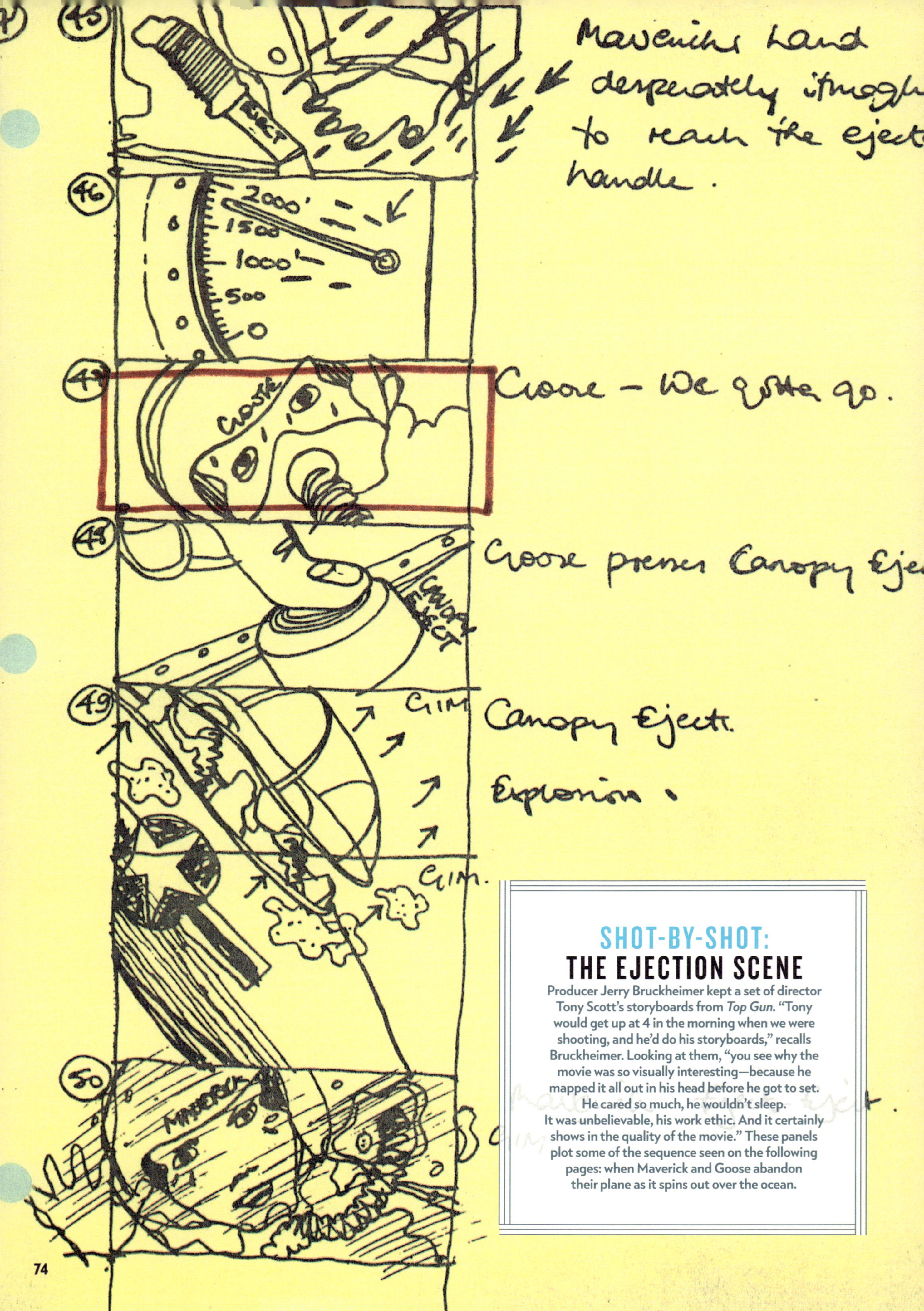

SHOT-BY-SHOT: THE EJECTION SCENE

Producer Jerry Bruckheimer kept a set of director Tony Scott's storyboards from *Top Gun*. "Tony would get up at 4 in the morning when we were shooting, and he'd do his storyboards," recalls Bruckheimer. Looking at them, "you see why the movie was so visually interesting—because he mapped it all out in his head before he got to set. He cared so much, he wouldn't sleep. It was unbelievable, his work ethic. And it certainly shows in the quality of the movie." These panels plot some of the sequence seen on the following pages: when Maverick and Goose abandon their plane as it spins out over the ocean.

51
GIM.
52
Canopy – held in slip
53
54
1000
55
MAVERICK
GIM.
Mav. – Eject Eject.
56
EJECTION
56A
57
Maverick Ejects.
GIM + BUILD.
58
Goose.
GIM + BUILD

AT SEA
Cruise and Edwards between takes of Goose's death scene (inset). Spoiler alert: This movie is 36 years old. You should have seen it by now.

"[FOR GOOSE] THEY WANTED A COMIC IN THAT ROLE, SOMEONE BROADER. THE THING ABOUT TONY IS . . . HE BROKE YOUR HEART"
—MARGERY SIMKIN, ON CASTING ANTHONY EDWARDS

> "WE SENT TOM THE SCRIPT . . . HE NEVER COMMITTED TO IT. I SAID 'I KNOW TOM LIKES MOTORCYCLES AND SPEED' SO WE GOT [THE NAVY] TO AGREE TO GIVE TOM A RIDE WITH THE BLUE ANGELS"
>
> **—JERRY BRUCKHEIMER**

HIS NEED FOR SPEED
Cruise's first Navy flight sealed the deal, says Bruckheimer. "They spun him and flipped him, made him deal with some heavy Gs. He got off the plane, wandered over to a pay phone , called me and said, 'I'm doing this.'"

ROMANTIC LEADS
"We were seeing the world for the Kelly part, I mean the *world*," says casting director Simkin. One reason McGillis, who had just appeared in *Witness*, won the role of Charlie came down to the director's vision. She adds: "I mean, Tony liked hot!"

FRIENDS AT THE END
Rick Rossovich (center, as Slider) recalls a mild rivalry between Kilmer and Cruise. "Val was pushing Tom. Val studied at Juilliard. He'd been Off-Broadway. He was beautiful to look at and talented as hell. Of course, Tom doesn't take it. He wouldn't take any prisoners."

"VAL AND I REALLY BONDED. WE BECAME BROTHERS. STILL ARE TO THIS DAY, EVEN THOUGH WE DON'T SEE EACH OTHER MUCH. I WAS HIS WING MAN, YOU CAN TAKE THAT ALL THE WAY"

—RICK ROSSOVICH, SLIDER

★ FROM THE *PEOPLE* VAULT ★

TOP GUN'S HOT NEW STAR

IN THE SUMMER OF 1986, *PEOPLE* SPENT TIME WITH TOM CRUISE FOR HIS SECOND BIG FEATURE STORY. HERE'S WHAT THE MAGAZINE—AND THE 23-YEAR-OLD ACTOR—SAID BACK THEN

TOM CRUISE WAS 21 years old when People *first devoted a feature story to the actor, in September 1983. (His first-ever mention in the magazine had been eight months earlier; it identified Cruise as Timothy Hutton's costar in the military academy drama* Taps.*) That was the year of his headlining role in* Risky Business, *in which Cruise slid on his white socks into moviegoers' hearts. "He occupies this movie the way Dustin Hoffman occupied* The Graduate,*" raved Roger Ebert. By 1986 Cruise had traded in his* Risky Business *Ray Bans for* Top Gun's *aviator shades and was about to rise to a different level of fame, kicking off an action-film career that has endured for more than three decades.*

For the story excerpted below, which originally ran June 2, 1986, People *caught up with Cruise in New York City. (A reminder: 1986 was a long, long time ago, when magazines turned phrases like "media morsel of the moment." Sorry, Tom!) But despite a bit of cringy-in-2022 language, the story captures a new star in his ascent. One who, by year's end, had even snarky critics reevaluating his potential, as he went head-to-head with Paul Newman in the Martin Scorsese-directed* The Color of Money. *(He did not, as the buzz back then predicted, earn an Oscar nod for that film, but he'd have one before the decade ended, for 1989's* Born on the Fourth of July.*) In short, the Cruise* People *spent time with was a busy, single and wildly successful young man on top of the world, kept grounded by family and homemade cookies.*

Screen

Cruise loved climbing into the cockpit for his *Top Gun* role. "Strong machines give me a real rush," he says.

IN THE RISKY BUSINESS OF BOX OFFICE AND BREAKING HEARTS, TOM CRUISE IS A NEW TOP GUN

Tom Cruise knows he's the media morsel of the moment. And, okay, it's great that his critically drubbed fly-boy flick, *Top Gun*, is off with a sensational $8.1 million opening weekend and that his critically decimated *Legend* was No. 1 at the box office three weeks running. "I have to smile about that," says Cruise, whose Christmas movie, *The Color of Money*, a *Hustler* sequel co-starring Paul Newman, is the one geared for Oscar nominations. But the fuss is beginning to make Cruise squirm. And on this sunny afternoon, he feels cramped in his Manhattan hotel suite (the Greenwich Village condo he bought last year is being redecorated). "I've been cooped up all day," he says, flashing his *Risky Business* grin. Tom wants to go lie in the grass in Central Park. "Let's hit it," he says.

So it's off to the park with the 23-year-old golden boy whom *Top Gun* director Tony Scott calls "a magnet for women." Before crossing the street, a fan requests an autograph. "Yes, sir," says Cruise, though the youth doing the asking is not much older than he. "Tom is frighteningly polite," says Scott. "He's so nice he's sick."

CONTINUED

WAY BACK
Above: *People* featured Cruise in a 1986 issue.

OPENING NIGHT
Right: Cruise attended *Top Gun's* New York City premiere May 12, 1986.

"
STRONG
MACHINES
GIVE ME
A REAL RUSH"
—TOM CRUISE,
TO *PEOPLE*,
ON THE THRILL
OF FILMING
TOP GUN

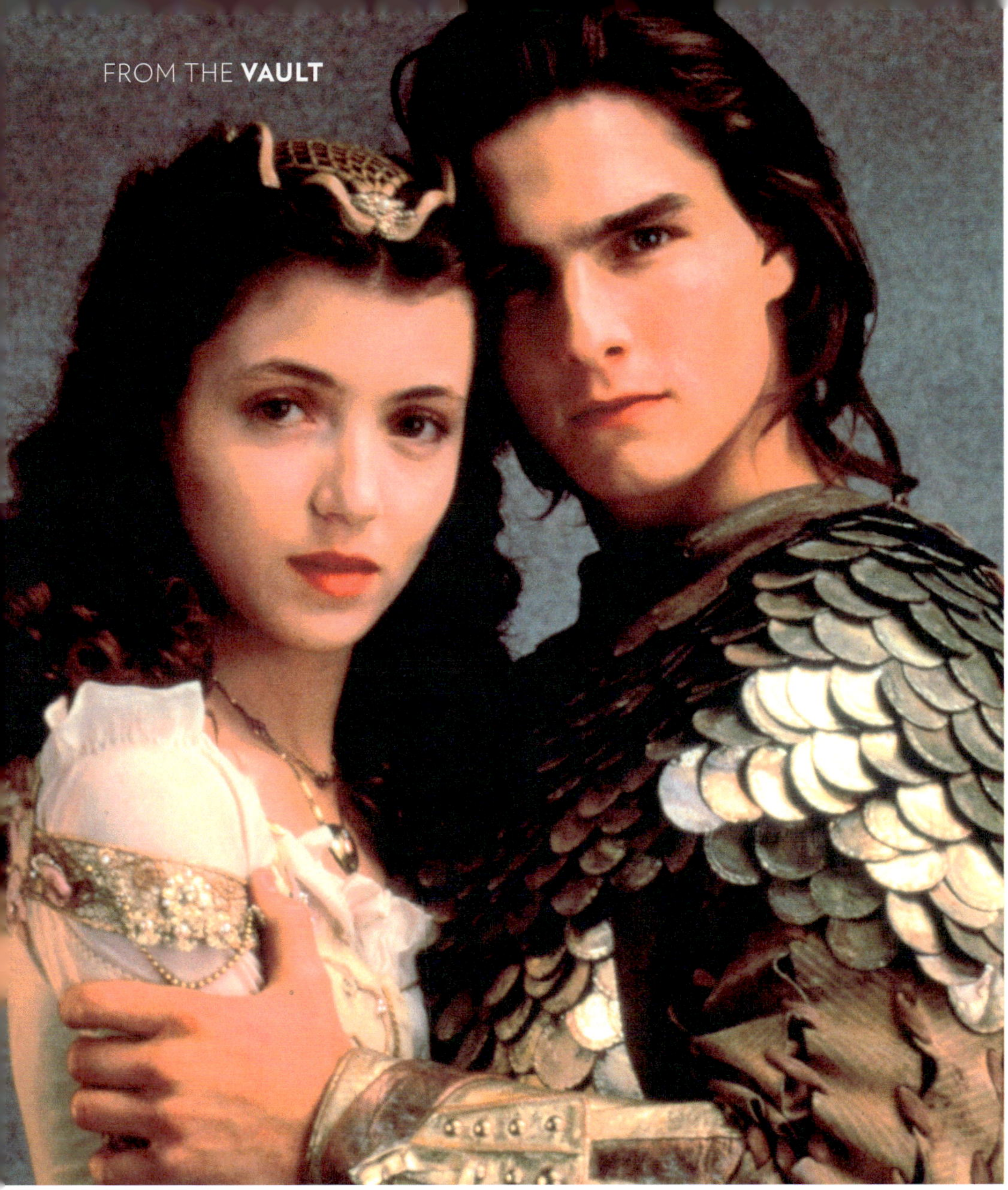

> "JUST BECAUSE *LEGEND* DIDN'T GET RAVES DOESN'T MEAN I LOVE IT LESS"
> **—CRUISE, 1986**

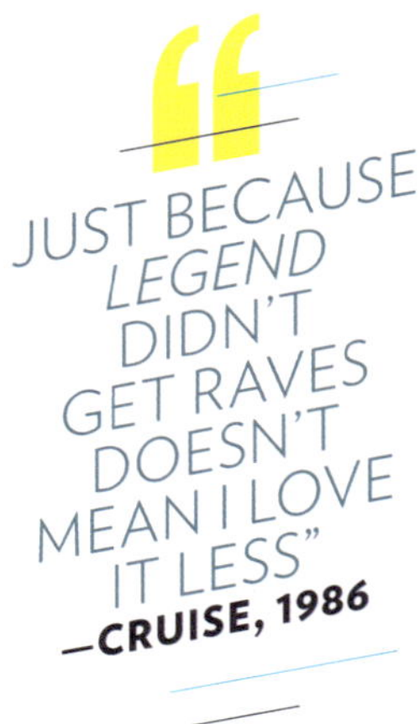

***LEGEND* IN HIS OWN TIME**
Left: Cruise played Jack o' the Green opposite Mia Sara as Princess Lili in Ridley Scott's 1985 fantasy film.

OUT WITH THE FAM
Right: At *Top Gun's* premiere, Cruise was joined by (from left) his sister Marian, cousin Tony and Tony's wife, Brenda, and grand-mother Comala.

Tom Cruise knows he's the media morsel of the moment. And, okay, it's great that his critically drubbed flyboy flick *Top Gun* is off with a sensational $8.1 million opening weekend and that his critically decimated *Legend* was No. 1 at the box office three weeks running. "I have to smile about that," says Cruise, whose Christmas movie *The Color of Money,* a *Hustler* sequel costarring Paul Newman, is the one geared for Oscar nominations. But the fuss is beginning to make Cruise squirm. And on this sunny afternoon, he feels cramped in his Manhattan hotel suite (the Greenwich Village condo he bought last year is being redecorated). "I've been cooped up all day," he says, flashing his *Risky Business* grin. Tom wants to go lie in the grass in Central Park. "Let's hit it," he says. So it's off to the park with the 23-year-old golden boy whom *Top Gun* director Tony Scott calls "a magnet for women." Before crossing the street, a fan requests an autograph. "Yes, sir," says Cruise, though the youth doing the asking is not much older than he. "Tom is frighteningly polite," says Scott. "He's so nice he's sick."

Flopping onto a spacious clump of grass, Cruise talks of wanting to be taken seriously. He didn't do *Top Gun* to become the summer's top pinup, though his oiled, muscled 5′9″ torso is prominently on display. "I wanted to make a piece about a character," he says. He even had a say in fleshing out the script. Cruise avoided socializing with costar Kelly McGillis (she plays his astrophysicist love) during early shooting to build sexual tension between the characters. "At first I thought this was corny actor bull," says director Scott. "But it worked."

To fine-tune his Navy pilot character, Cruise took three hops in an F-14 fighter jet. "Those jets [climbing 30,000 ft. in a minute] rip through the clouds," says Cruise. "It's very sexual. Your body contorts, your muscles get sore, and the straining forces blood from your brain. You grab your legs and your ass and grunt as the sweat pours over you. It's just thrilling.

I had this grin on my face that wouldn't leave."

Talk of his heartthrob image has him grinning too. Ever since he and *Risky Business* costar Rebecca De Mornay split, Tom has been rumored cruising everyone from McGillis and Lori Singer to older woman Cher. "Not true," he protests. Tom met Cher last year. "She's funny and bright, and we're good buddies and that's it," he says. Then he relates a story: "A friend said, 'I hear you went out with Daryl Hannah.' I said, 'I did? How was I?' I had never met her. I don't know why people think I'm running around with everybody." For all that, Cruise makes no claims to celibacy. That went out after one year of studying to be a priest at a Franciscan seminary. "I date women," he says, without volunteering names. "And I like women. I grew up in a house full of them."

Born in Syracuse, N.Y., Tom and his three sisters lived in Canada, Cincinnati and St. Louis, as his father, an electrical engineer, moved from job to job. When Tom was 11, his parents divorced, and Mom and the kids settled in Kentucky. Five years later she married a plastics salesman, and the family relocated in Glen Ridge, N.J. Tom, who is dyslexic, threw himself into sports. It was a way of making friends. Sidelined by a high school wrestling injury, he tried acting in a school production. He preferred emoting to enrolling in college, moved to New York and bussed tables until he won a bit part in 1981's *Endless Love.* That led to *Taps, The Outsiders* and *Losin' It* before hitting the jackpot with *Risky Business.*

His career kept him a nomad, living in rentals or with pals like Sean Penn and Emilio Estevez. Until now. The condo is the first place he's owned. At around a million per film, he can afford it. But don't expect extravagance. He invests. Tom's sister Cass joined him on a recent vacation to Hawaii, but they flew coach. "My sisters take good care of me," he adds. "They send cookies." **—DAVID HUTCHINGS**

"HE WAS LIKE AN ADMIRAL, THE WAY HE COMMANDED THE TROOPS. THEY LOVED HIM. HE KNEW EVERY CREW MEMBER'S NAME—HUNDREDS"
—JERRY BRUCKHEIMER

★ *TOP GUN'S* DIRECTOR ★

REMEMBERING TONY SCOTT

HE CREATED BLOCKBUSTERS AND CULT FILMS ALIKE—AND, WITH BROTHER RIDLEY, MADE EVEN MORE HITS FOR TV AND FILM. HIS 2012 DEATH LEFT HOLLYWOOD SHOCKED AND FRIENDS BEREFT

TOM CRUISE RECALLED a day when *Top Gun's* director ordered an aircraft carrier repositioned off the coast of San Diego, so the light in a single shot would be just so. The admiral in charge balked at the cost. But, said Cruise in a 2012 *Time* remembrance after Tony Scott's death at age 68, "Tony pulled out his checkbook right there and wrote a check for $25,000 to pay for the fuel. He was right too. The light wasn't right."

Born in the North of England, Anthony Scott began his cinematic journey in the mid-'60s, acting in a student film for older brother Ridley, who would soon establish himself as a top helmer of British TV commercials. Ridley recruited Tony, by then an art-school grad, to join his stable of directors, which led to a first feature film, *The Hunger* (1983), a high-toned vampire tale starring Susan Sarandon, Catherine Deneuve and David Bowie that received a cool reception in its time but has become a cult favorite. If some in Hollywood were snobbish about commercial directors jumping to feature films, producers Jerry Bruckheimer and Don Simpson were not—they liked what they saw in an ad Scott had directed, in which a sports car races a fighter jet, and sought him out for *Top Gun*. (Ridley Scott, who directed Cruise in *Legend*, released in the U.S. the same year, had urged the actor and his brother to work together.) Scott's follow-up films included sequels (*Beverly Hills Cop II,* with Eddie Murphy), redos (*The Taking of Pelham 1 2 3,* one of five films he made with Denzel Washington), white-knuckle action (*Enemy of the State,* with Will Smith) and a pulp-crime (*True Romance,* written by Quentin Tarantino).

Scott's interest in thrills extended offscreen: He had a passion for mountain climbing and motorcycles. He reteamed with Cruise for the NASCAR film *Days of Thunder* in 1990. On that set he met actress Donna Wilson; the couple married in 1994 and had twin sons, Frank and Max. Scott was known for intense dedication to his projects. Bruckheimer, his partner on six films, says, "You can compare him to [NFL coach] Bill Belichick, a guy who works like crazy to win every game. Tony worked the hardest and cared the most."

It came as a shock to colleagues and fans when, on Aug. 19, 2012, Scott died by suicide, leaping from a bridge over the Los Angeles Harbor. "He had a tremendous passion for life and for the art of filmmaking and was able to share this passion with all of us," said Denzel Washington. Cruise added to the chorus of grief, saying, "Tony was my dear friend, and I will really miss him. He was a creative visionary whose mark on film is immeasurable." —**ERIK FORREST JACKSON**

ORIGINAL MOTION PICTURE

KENNY LOGGINS
DANGER ZONE
LOVERBOY
HEAVEN IN YOUR EYES
CHEAP TRICK
MIGHTY WINGS
BERLIN
TAKE MY BREATH AWAY
(LOVE THEME FROM "TOP GUN")
HAROLD FALTERMEYER
& STEVE STEVENS
TOP GUN ANTHEM

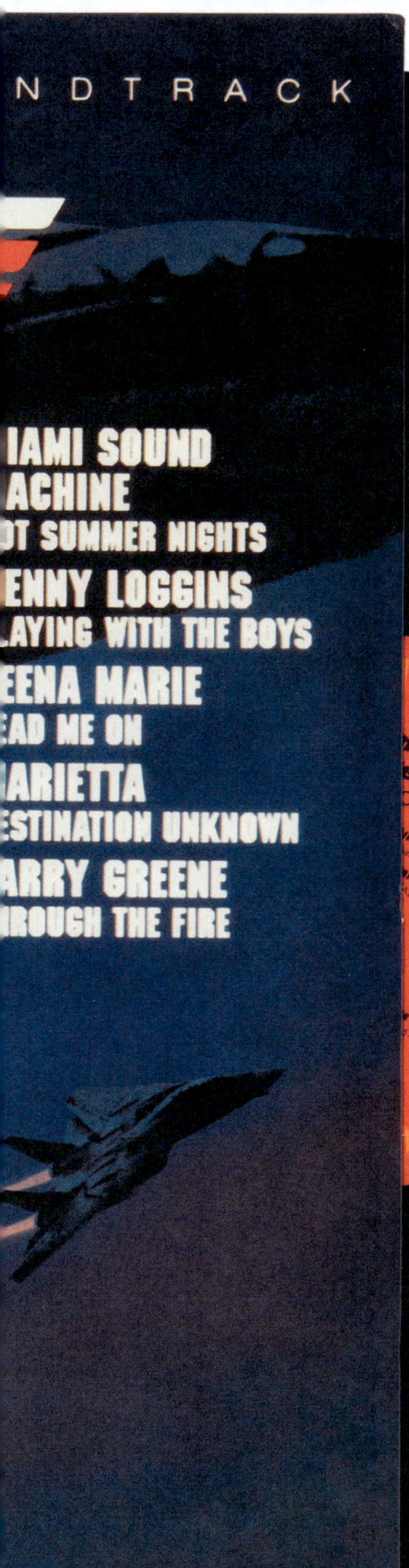

★ THE ALBUM ★

SOUND OF THE SKIES

EVEN IF YOU NEVER SET FOOT IN A MULTIPLEX IN 1986, YOU COULDN'T MISS THE YEAR'S TOP SOUNDTRACK, FULL OF NO. 1 HITS AND AN OSCAR WIN

Top Gun's soundtrack went multiplatinum and was a prime expression of 1980s movie music: booming, heavily orchestrated—even over-the-top. Along with a score by Harold Faltermeyer and original songs by Giorgio Moroder, the film throbs to the beat of pop tunes spanning three decades—from the Righteous Brothers and Otis Redding to REO Speedwagon and the Miami Sound Machine, making *Top Gun* a driving, pulsating aural experience.

BERLIN
TAKE MY BREATH AWAY

Film producers had rejected numerous artists proposed to sing *Top Gun's* love theme, until songwriter Giorgio Moroder suggested a new wave group he was producing, Berlin. "He said, 'I'm working with this band… and they are going to be big,'" recalls lead singer Terri Nunn (above, in 1987 with bandmates Rob Brill, left, and John Crawford). "He was always a real promoter. And they're like, 'Do it then, because we need *somebody*.'" At first, however, Nunn didn't find the tune—at least as Moroder played it—sufficiently romantic. "So I actually had the balls to sing it in a different way," she tells *People* today. "I changed the melody, elongated it, and I f---ed around with it. And they loved it. It was a complete shock." The smoldering ballad set the mood for the love scenes between Tom Cruise and Kelly McGillis and went on to become a certified gold single and win the Academy Award for Best Original Song.

GUNNING FOR THE GOLD Moroder (right, in '87 with lyricist Tom Whitlock) is a founding father of disco.

KENNY LOGGINS
DANGER ZONE

The song became a staple of Loggins's act. But he wasn't on anyone's list to perform Moroder's high-adrenaline theme until Bryan Adams and Toto, among others, didn't work out. Loggins figured it was worth a shot—no matter how *Top Gun* fared. "There's no guarantee a movie's going to be any kind of success," Loggins says, "so at the very least you want to come out of it with a great song and maybe some traction on the radio."

THE RIGHTEOUS BROTHERS
YOU'VE LOST THAT LOVIN' FEELIN'

Top Gun fans know this bluesy lament from the bar scene in which Tom Cruise and Anthony Edwards serenade Kelly McGillis. The 1964 Phil Spector/Barry Mann/Cynthia Weil composition is consistently ranked among the greatest pop songs of all time, a prime example of producer Spector's dense "wall of sound" recording technique. It was also a signature No. 1 hit for blue-eyed soul duo the Righteous Brothers, showcasing Bill Medley's (top at left) booming bass-baritone and Bobby Hatfield's stratospheric falsetto.

riusxm

★ INTERVIEW ★

KENNY LOGGINS BACK IN THE DANGER ZONE

THE SINGER-SONGWRITER'S RANGY TENOR WAS A DEFINING SOUND OF '70S AND '80S POP RADIO. NOW HE'S REPRISING *TOP GUN*'S POWERHOUSE HIT

BY RICHARD JEROME

King of the Soundtracks. That's what they called Kenny Loggins in the '80s, when you could hear his voice in *Caddyshack* ("I'm Alright"), *Footloose* (title track) and *Top Gun*'s driving, pulsating "Danger Zone." Of course, Loggins had long been part of the soundtrack of real life, through his work with the Nitty Gritty Dirt Band, his partnership with Jim Messina and a long solo career. Hits such as "This Is It," "Whenever I Call You Friend" and "What a Fool Believes" are pop perennials. For *Top Gun,* Loggins had recorded his own composition "Playing With the Boys" and was later given "Danger Zone." Now Loggins, who still makes music (and occasionally plays himself on *Family Guy*), has recorded a new version of that signature song for *Maverick*. He spoke with *People* about his long relationship with the *Top Gun* hit.

So, how did you wind up singing 'Danger Zone'?

LOGGINS I just wanted to be part of the soundtrack and cut "Playing With the Boys" (which scores the volleyball scene) as part of an open call for pop acts. That was a slam dunk. Later I got a call that they needed a singer for one of Giorgio Moroder's songs. The only thing I asked was "Is it an up-tempo?" because I needed a rocker for my live show. I got together with Giorgio and lyricist Tom Whitlock, and we changed a few words and a few chords. Next day I was in the studio, it went great, and suddenly it's "Danger Zone."

You've said that because you didn't write it, the song wasn't something you felt much for—you just had fun with it.

The primary lyric was just "highway to the danger zone." At first I thought, "Well, maybe that's oversimplified." But when you see it against the scene, it's obvious the only thing they want to convey is the courage it takes to fly those planes. So you just send that message home. I was listening to a lot of Tina Turner, and I was imitating Tina to get that rock edge to it.

The military said your music video was a great recruiting tool.

Yes, but I was disappointed, to put it mildly, that CNN used "Danger Zone" to show footage of us bombing Iraq. That was never my intention, to sing a theme song to a scene of death and destruction.

As for *Maverick*—were you going for a different feeling this time? The song is so quintessentially '80s.

No, I went for a duplication of the original as much as possible, only now using different recording techniques. Now theaters have the sound coming from all around you, so that has to be recorded differently. The original was just stereo that kind of sounds like a mono. So I wanted bigger drums and bigger guitar sounds but essentially the same sounds booming around the theater.

So now a song you didn't plan on has been a Loggins standard for decades.

A real identity piece. It was providential.

EVERYTHING OLD IS NEW AGAIN
Loggins hasn't seen his "Danger Zone" video "in forever. There's a lot of that stuff my kids have never seen and my girlfriend's never seen; she'd never heard of me when I met her."

STEVE STEVENS & HAROLD FALTERMEYER
TOP GUN ANTHEM

Faltermeyer was noodling around with a tune for the Chevy Chase comedy *Fletch* when his pal Billy Idol, rehearsing next door, dropped by. "He said, 'Harold, that's great... you should use it for *Top Gun,*'" Faltermeyer (also known for "Axel F," the synth-heavy theme from *Beverly Hills Cop*) recalled. The composer not only took the advice to heart but enlisted Idol's lead guitarist, Steve Stevens, to create the stirring hard-rock "Top Gun Anthem," which opens the movie. It turned out to be a great gig for Stevens, winning him and Faltermeyer a Grammy for Best Pop Instrumental Performance.

JERRY LEE LEWIS
GREAT BALLS OF FIRE

Otis Blackwell and Jack Hammer's rockabilly classic—popularized by Lewis in the 1957 film *Jamboree*—got the barroom treatment when Anthony Edwards bangs the ivories and belts it with Cruise, McGillis and Meg Ryan. When director Tony Scott suggested it, "I was like, 'Tony, I don't play piano, I don't sing, and I don't know the song,'" Edwards told *Access Hollywood.* "He said, 'Great, we'll meet you there with a piano teacher and voice guy.' We dove in, and by 10 o'clock we were shooting."

ANTHEM ROCK
Above: Faltermeyer at the 1987 Grammy Awards. Left: Steve Stevens.

CREDITS

FRONT COVER
Paramount Pictures; (inset) Paramount Pictures/Photofest

20 Everett(2); **21** Kevin Winter/Getty Images; **38** Tom Stratton; **39** Gary Miller/Getty Images; **40** Everett; **41** Austin Hargrave/August; **56-57** (from left) Jessica Chou/Redux Pictures; Hannes Magerstaedt/Getty Images; **66** (from top) Ron Galella/Ron Galella Collection/Getty Images; Kevin Winter/DMI/The LIFE Picture Collection/Getty Images; **71** (right, from top) Alamy; Courtesy Judy Scholl; **83** Ron Galella/Ron Galella Collection/Getty Images; **84** Snap/Shutterstock; **85** Ron Galella/Ron Galella Collection/Getty Images; **86-87** Everett; **88-89** Peter Ardito; **90** (from top) Dave Hogan/Hulton Archive/Getty Images; Ron Galella/Ron Galella Collection/Getty Images; **91** (bottom) Chris Walter/WireImage/Getty Images; **92** Steven Ferdman/Getty Images; **93** Michael Ochs Archives/Getty Images; **94** (clockwise from top left) Fred Sabine/NBCU Photo Bank/NBCUniversal/Getty Images; Michael Ochs Archives/Getty Images; Ebet Roberts/Redferns/Getty Images; **96** (clockwise from left) Shutterstock; Ross Marino/Getty Images; Jeffrey R. Staab/CBS/Getty Images; Val Wilmer/Redferns/Getty Images; Everett; Hulton Archive/Getty Images; Michael Ochs Archives/Getty Images; David Mcgough/DMI/The LIFE Picture Collection/Shutterstock; James Schnepf/Getty Images; Silver Screen Collection/Getty Images

All other photos Courtesy Paramount Pictures

PEOPLE
President Leah Wyar
Editor Liz Vaccariello
Creative Director Andrea Dunham
Director of Photography Ilana Schweber
Director of Editorial Operations Alexandra Brez

PEOPLE BOOKS
Editor Allison Adato
Art Director Greg Monfries
Photo Editor C. Tiffany Lee
Contributing Photo Editor Louis Pearlman
Writers Rebecca Ascher-Walsh, Eileen Finan, Erik Forrest Jackson, Richard Jerome, Chris Nashawaty
Deputy Art Director Ronnie Brandwein-Keats
Reporters Gillian Aldrich, Stewart Allen, Mary Hart
Copy Desk Joanann Scali (Chief), James Bradley (Deputy), Ellen Adamson, Gabrielle Danchick, Rich Donnelly, Matt Weingarden (Copy Editors)
Production Designers Lori Cervone, Peter Niceberg
Premedia Imaging Specialist David Swain
Color Quality Analysts Sara Luckey, Rob Roszkowski
PEOPLE Public Relations Marnie Perez, Julie Farin

DOTDASH MEREDITH PREMIUM PUBLISHING
Vice President & General Manager Jeremy Biloon
Vice President, Group Editorial Director Stephen Orr
Director, Brand Marketing Jean Kennedy
Associate Director, Brand Marketing Bryan Christian
Senior Brand Manager Katherine Barnet

Editorial Director Kostya Kennedy
Creative Director Gary Stewart
Director of Photography Christina Lieberman
Editorial Operations Director Jamie Roth Major
Manager, Editorial Operations Gina Scauzillo
Special thanks Brad Beatson, Samantha Lebofsky, Kate Roncinske, Céline Wojtala

DIGITAL
President Leah Wyar
VP/Group General Manager People Zoe Ruderman

1. MILES TELLER
'BOB SEGER'S "OLD TIME ROCK & ROLL."'
"It's a jukebox kind of song. Even if people aren't into rock and roll, Seger can get them dancing."

★ THE *TOP GUN* TOP 10 ★

WHAT THE STARS SING IN BARS

THE *MAVERICK* CAST REVEAL THEIR GO-TO KARAOKE TUNES

2. JON HAMM
"I'd go with something from Prince. Definitely an artist that everyone can get behind. There's no bad Prince song."

3. JENNIFER CONNELLY
"For my daughter's music class, we had to do a rendition of Beyoncé's 'Halo.' A song like that really demonstrates what a great singer she is. And the disparity between her voice [and mine]."

4. BASHIR SALAHUDDIN
"'Luck Be a Lady' by Frank Sinatra. [*Singing*] *'A lady doesn't wander all over the room and blow on some other guy's dice.'* Tons of innuendo, a crowd pleaser."

5. ED HARRIS
"Boy, it would have to be a Dylan tune. Maybe 'Mr. Tambourine Man.'"

6. JAY ELLIS
"'Welcome to New York City' by Jay-Z. Or—a guilty pleasure—Whitney Houston's 'I Wanna Dance With Somebody.' It's a classic. No one can be wrong singing that song."

7. GLEN POWELL
"'Friends in Low Places' by Garth Brooks, a favorite of mine. And over the course of this press tour I also want to bust out 'Leaving on a Jet Plane' or 'You've Lost That Lovin' Feelin'.' It would be a crime if the cast didn't do those somewhere. Singing in bars is very much a part of *Top Gun*."

8. CHARLES PARNELL
"Prince, Stevie Wonder or Bob Marley. Those are three of my favorite artists, so something in one of those catalogs."

9. LEWIS PULLMAN
"'Dancing in the Dark' by Bruce Springsteen. There's nothing else for me. I wish I could change it up, but I'm chained to that song. It's all in the hips. And it's just a pendulum, and it happens, and it can't be stopped."

10. MONICA BARBARO
"'Blame It on the Boogie' by the Jacksons. I know every word and every little nuance of vocal accentuation in the song. In our main training aircraft we were allowed to play music, and the instructor insisted that flying is rock and roll, but I made him listen to disco for hours. I guess I'm fueled by fun!"

Made in United States
Cleveland, OH
26 July 2025

18873186R00059